Shroud
OF THE Lion

Children's Books by
Sigmund Brouwer
FROM BETHANY HOUSE PUBLISHERS

THE ACCIDENTAL DETECTIVES

The Volcano of Doom
The Disappearing Jewel of Madagascar
Legend of the Gilded Saber
Tyrant of the Badlands
Shroud of the Lion
Creature of the Mists

WATCH OUT FOR JOEL!

Bad Bug Blues
Long Shot
Camp Craziness
Fly Trap

www.coolreading.com

Accidental
DETECTIVES

Shroud
OF THE Lion

SIGMUND BROUWER

BETHANYHOUSE
MINNEAPOLIS, MINNESOTA

Shroud of the Lion
Copyright © 2003
Sigmund Brouwer

Author's Note: Griffin Park is loosely based on Griffith Park.

Cover illustration by Chris Ellison
Cover design by Lookout Design Group, Inc.

Published by Bethany House Publishers
11400 Hampshire Avenue South
Bloomington, Minnesota 55438
www.bethanyhouse.com

Bethany House Publishers is a Division of
Baker Book House Company, Grand Rapids, Michigan.

Printed in the United States of America

Library of Congress Cataloging-in-Publication Data

Brouwer, Sigmund, 1959-
    Shroud of the lion / by Sigmund Brouwer.
        p. cm. — (Accidental detectives)
Summary: As they set out to be extras in a Hollywood movie, Ricky and his friends face danger and difficult faith questions.
    ISBN 0-7642-2568-5 (pbk.)
    [1. Mystery and detective stories. 2. Lions—Fiction. 3. Christian life—Fiction. 4. Los Angeles (Calif.)—Fiction.] I. Title. II. Series: Brouwer, Sigmund, 1959-   . Accidental detectives.
    PZ7.B79984Sh   2003
    [Fic]—dc21
                                                                    2003001932

SIGMUND BROUWER is the award-winning author of scores of books. He speaks to kids around the continent in an effort to instill good reading and writing habits in the next generation. Sigmund and his wife, Cindy Morgan, divide their time between Tennessee and Alberta, Canada.

For Olivia
and the sunshine you bring
into this world

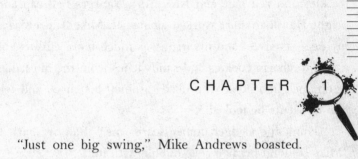

CHAPTER 1

"Just one big swing," Mike Andrews boasted. "That's all it's going to take for a brute like me."

I was on my knees in front of him, holding a large nail in place on top of a chopping block that was normally used for splitting logs.

It was a Saturday afternoon in early summer, the kind of Saturday that you daydream about during the last month of school. Clear blue sky, slight breeze. Cheerfully chirping birds. And nothing much to do here in Mike's backyard except listen to the sounds of a growing argument mix with the chirping around us.

"Brute?" Ralphy Zee stood beside me and spoke to Mike. "You're so wimpy that when a kid on a tricycle passes, the breeze knocks you over. It would take you a dozen swings, but you'd tire out before the first ten."

"Ralphy," I warned. "Remember what Mike's got in his hands."

Kneeling in front of the chopping block, I sure wasn't about to forget. It was a sledgehammer. With a twenty-pound head.

Mike lifted it with a grunt and gave Ralphy an evil grin. He might have been trying to look tough and scary, but his freckles and red hair and New York Yankees ball cap and bright Hawaiian shirt worked against it. Mike Andrew was my age—twelve—and his grin was much more effective as a tool to charm cookies and sandwiches from the old ladies in our neighborhood who liked to pinch his cheek and tell him how cute he looked.

"Think the sledgehammer scares me?" Ralphy snarled. "Mike couldn't break a soap bubble with it."

Not that Ralphy's snarl was much to scare anybody, either. Ralphy was our resident computer guy. He had the pasty white skin of someone who spends hours in front of a keyboard and screen. And the lack of muscles that goes with it, too. He had mousy brown hair that a comb could never conquer, and I'd never seen him with his shirt completely tucked in. If Mike was a charmer, Ralphy was the lovable, messy, distracted genius.

"Soap bubble?" Mike echoed. "I'm telling you, one big swing is all it's going to take. Right, Richard Kidd?"

Whenever Mike called me by my full name, he was serious.

"Sure," I said with a sigh, not impressed. "Whatever you say. Can you guys just get this over with? I've decided I want to get away from your endless talk."

"Need to go home for a nap?" Ralphy said, still trying to sound tough. "Little boy sleepy?"

As a matter of fact, I wasn't little. I was a shade tall for my age and had the same blondish hair as my dad. I preferred books to computers but spent as much time in sports as I did in reading. Even though it was hot, I was wearing a long-sleeved shirt, and I felt uncomfortable in it. I usually wore a T-shirt with jeans.

"Tell you what," I told Ralphy, sighing again. "You want to hold the nail for Mike? Or are you scared?"

Unnecessary as it was, I pointed with my left hand. My right hand was balanced on the big chopping block. There was a six-inch nail pinched between the thumb and forefinger, ready for Mike to drive into the wood with his sledgehammer.

"I'm not scared," Ralphy answered. "But you're the one who said you could pull your hand away in time."

"Fine," I said. "Just remember. If Mike drives the nail all the way in with one swing, you have to mow each of our lawns for the next two weeks."

Ralphy snorted. "As long as you remember when he needs more than one swing that you guys will be mowing my lawn for the entire summer."

"Yeah, yeah," I said. "Mike, you ready?"

He lifted the sledgehammer high above his head. "Ready."

"Hang on," I said. "I just want to get this straight. It's on the count of three, right?"

"Right," Mike said. He set the sledgehammer down. It was so big and heavy that he wasn't able to hold it above his head for long. "One, two, three, and then swing."

He lifted it again. "One—"

"Hang on," I said.

Mike slowly lowered the sledgehammer.

I continued, "I'd rather you counted 'one' and 'two' and swung as you said 'three.' Not after 'three.'"

"But—"

"It's my hand," I said. "I want to be exactly sure when I should pull it away."

"Fine," Mike said. He lifted the sledgehammer high again. "One . . . two—"

"Hang on," I said again.

"What now?" He set the sledgehammer down, panting slightly.

"Don't get grumpy," I said. "It's not like we've ever had a chance to practice this. I'm just thinking maybe I should count. That way you can concentrate on hitting the nail. And I'll know exactly when to pull my hand away."

"I know, I know," he said. "It's your hand."

"Exactly."

One more time Mike brought the sledgehammer up. He waited, ready to slam it down on the nail.

"One . . ." I said. I took a breath. "Mike, make sure you don't miss."

"Yeah, yeah," he said. "Get to two and three."

"Going to start over," I said. "Just to make sure there's no confusion."

"I can't hold this hammer up here forever, pal."

"One . . ." I said. "Two . . ."

Mike swung down as hard as he could.

In a blur, the sledgehammer dropped from the sky.

Thump! Twenty pounds of sledgehammer head smashed into the chopping block.

And onto the fingers holding the spike. Red mush splattered everywhere. The splat of impact was drowned out by the thump of the sledgehammer.

And by my scream.

I screamed again. Again, and again.

"Mike," I shouted when I could find words. "You were supposed to wait for three! Not on two. On three!"

"I got too excited," he moaned. "Sorry!"

"Sorry?" I screamed again. "Look at my finger on the ground! Broken bone!"

Sure enough, the chalky white end of bone was plain to see. Sticking out from meat and blood.

"I'll get it," Mike said. "We can put it in a bag and—"

A small brown dog ran up and snatched the finger away before Mike could stoop over to pick it up.

"Oooh," Ralphy said. "I'm going to be . . ."

He sagged to his knees, fell over on his back, and then threw up on the front of his shirt. Another small dog ran up to him, jumped on his chest, and began to lap away at the mess.

A few seconds later, Lisa Higgins stepped up to Ralphy and stared down at him. My little brother, Joel, followed her and reached down to pet the dog's head as it ate.

"Perfect," Lisa said. "Absolutely perfect."

CHAPTER  2

"That was fun," I told Lisa as I got up from my knees and stepped away from the chopping block. "Do you think I overdid the screaming?"

"I don't think anyone could scream too loud after something like that," she answered. She rewarded me with a smile.

Her smile was like the sun breaking through clouds. Lisa Higgins lived a few houses down from me in our small town of Jamesville. She had dark hair and a flash temper. But I'd never seen her get angry unless somebody deserved it. Like when Mike or Ralphy or I made the mistake of thinking that she couldn't do something just because she was a girl.

"Did you get it all?" I asked. "I mean, the right hand is totally gone. I'd hate to think all of this work was wasted."

Bits and pieces of it were still on top of the chopping block, sticky with red goo and meaty material.

"Yeah," Ralphy said. "Remember all the time we spent getting ready for this."

"I remember," Lisa said. "Trust me, I remember. You guys argued the whole time over who got to swing the sledgehammer and smash it."

Mike was ignoring us. He bent over to pick something up from the grass.

"Another finger," he said, inspecting it. "The dumb dog missed it."

Mike held the finger up and snapped it. The crack was very clear, and it exposed more white bone. He whistled for the first dog to come back. When it did, he dropped the finger, and the dog ran away with it to the corner of the yard.

"Come on," Ralphy said, trying to sit up. "Someone help me with this thing."

Ralphy tried to push the other dog off his chest. It whined and stayed squarely on him.

"Joel!" Ralphy said. "Please!"

My little brother waved for the dog. It jumped off Ralphy and into Joel's arms and started licking Joel's face. Which was why we'd brought Joel along for this. He was six years younger than I was, and he had a magical touch with animals.

Ralphy stood. He wiped some of the mess off his chest, then sucked his fingers clean. "Not bad," he said. "Maybe I'll ask Mom to serve it tonight for supper."

The right sleeve of my shirt flapped at my wrist. I buttoned it.

"Well, gentlemen," Lisa said, "we've got a little more work to do. Then give me until next Saturday, and I'll show you a masterpiece."

Deliberately risking getting your hand pounded with a sledgehammer is not smart. But at least if you ever did smash your hand beyond repair—on purpose or accidentally—you could still live through life with a damaged hand, or even, scary as the thought is, without a hand at all.

But your brain is a different matter.

Without it, you're dead.

With a damaged brain—depending on the kind of damage—life can be extremely difficult or even impossible.

I don't think anyone would argue with that. Stupid as it is to risk damaging your hand, it's even stupider to risk hurting your brain.

Not many kids would let their heads get near a moving sledgehammer. But sometimes they'll think about putting their brains in the way of something that can do at least as much damage as a sledgehammer, just a little more slowly.

That something is drugs. Drugs to get high.

Drugs definitely aren't cool.

That was all we wanted to show by what we did on that Saturday afternoon.

We just didn't realize where all of that work would lead us. Or how truly dangerous it would become.

And all of it began with Lisa and her masterpiece.

CHAPTER 3

"You are not going to believe it," Lisa said. "You are absolutely not going to believe it."

Now that it was the following Saturday afternoon, all of us were gathered in the living room at my house. Lisa had arrived on time as promised.

"Believe what?" Ralphy asked.

"No," she said, "first the masterpiece. Then I'm going to tell you what you won't believe. And trust me, you're going to want to believe it."

"Believe what?" Ralphy said again.

"First the masterpiece." Lisa handed me a DVD, and I turned to the television and slid the disc into our DVD player.

"Of course," Lisa said, "I hope none of you have any serious plans for next week."

"Come on," Ralphy said. "What?"

"You're not going to believe it," Lisa answered. "Just won't believe it."

Mike groaned. "If you weren't going to tell us, why bring it up in the first place?"

Lisa gave us her mysterious, beautiful smile.

"Because I'm a girl."

"I hate gender stereotyping," Mike muttered. "It's such a convenient excuse for shallow behavior. I don't understand why she can't just tell us."

"Mike," I said, "there's a simple solution here."

"What?"

I waved the remote control at Mike. "We view the masterpiece."

First I closed the large curtains on the large living room window. It made the room as dim as a movie theater. Mike and Ralphy and Joel sat on the couch. Lisa and I stood behind them.

"Ready?" I asked Lisa.

"Ready."

I hit the Play button on the remote. Beautiful symphony music played as the screen went from dark to showing Mike's backyard. The view panned the trees and a small garden. Then it stopped in the corner of the yard, where Mike and Ralphy and I were at the chopping block.

"Nice touch," I whispered to Lisa. "Elegant music contrasted against something as grim as a chopping block."

"Thought you'd like it," she whispered back.

There was a close-up of Mike holding the sledgehammer.

Then a longer shot with all three of us in the frame again, me kneeling at the chopping block.

Mike's voice was clear as the camera shot a close-up of his face. *"Just one big swing. That's all it's going to take for a brute like me."*

Ralphy's answer was just as clear. *"Brute? You're so wimpy that when a kid on a tricycle passes, the breeze knocks you over. It would—"*

"Was that the third take?" Ralphy asked Lisa. "I thought the third take was my best."

"Shhhh," Mike said.

The camera angles shifted as each of us talked. I was fascinated by how it seemed to flow smoothly, even though Lisa had stood behind a video camera on a tripod and made each of us say our lines separately at least ten times. She'd done a lot of work splicing it together to make it seem as natural as the way it had happened on the final take when we did it one last time before Mike swung the hammer down.

That had been the crucial shot. Where Lisa had lined up five borrowed video cameras all on tripods to capture the action five different ways.

And as it unfolded on the television screen in front of us, it was obvious that it had been worth the preparation and effort.

"One . . . Mike, make sure you don't miss."

Close-up of the sledgehammer above his head.

"Yeah, yeah. Get to two and three."

Quick shot of the chopping block and my right hand holding the nail.

"Going to start over. Just to make sure there's no confusion."

Quick shot of my face.

"I can't hold this hammer up here forever, pal."

Quick shot of Mike's face. The symphony music continued to play softly in the background.

"One ... two ..."

Then slow-motion shots of the hammer coming down. From three different angles. Lisa had done a bunch of takes of that to finish the day. Watching it here, it seemed like all of them had been shot during Mike's first swing.

The music stopped for the thump of the sledgehammer against the chopping block.

Then came my screams. Loud at first, then fading. A quick shot of the sledgehammer missing the nail and hitting the fingers. Then a slow-motion shot of the same thing. A quick shot of my face in agony. All with my screaming in the background.

"Mike! You were supposed to wait for three. Not on two. On three!"

"I got too excited. Sorry!"

"Sorry? Look at my finger on the ground! Broken bone!"

A quick shot of a finger lying on the ground, with the chalky white bone sticking out.

"I'll get it. We can put it in a bag and—"

A quick shot of the dog running up and snatching away the finger.

Then shots of all the rest that followed. Ralphy falling over. Throwing up. A dog running onto his chest and eating the mess on his shirt.

The symphony music swelled as the camera closed in on the chopping block one final time. With the nail on its side on top of the block. The nail that Mike had missed with his gigantic blow.

And as the screen faded to black and the music died down, a female voice—Lisa's—spoke slowly and clearly:

"Think that was dumb? But even they wouldn't try drugs."

Then silence.

In the darkness of the living room, all of us began to applaud.

"Great commercial," I said to Lisa. "It really works, doesn't it."

"I like the way it captured my character," Mike said. "Grim, determined, and yet optimistic in a very postmodern way. I really felt I portrayed all of it very effectively with just a few simple facial movements."

"Play it again," Ralphy said. "Play it again!"

I stepped over to the living room window and pulled open the curtains.

"Lisa's got copies," I told Ralphy. "You can watch it as many times as you like. At your house. Later. Because Lisa has something unbelievable to tell us. Right, Lisa?"

"Right," she said.

She began to pace back and forth, tapping her chin with the forefinger of her right hand.

"Let me start by telling you I thought it was great work by all of you. It—"

"Lisa," I interrupted. "We're dying here. What is it that we're not going to believe that we're going to want to believe?"

"Let me put it this way," she said. "Ever been to Holly-wood?"

"Hollywood!" we all said at once.

"There's a famous actor who has invited all of us to visit him on location as he films a movie."

"No way!" Mike said.

"Yes way." Lisa smiled.

"All of us?" I asked.

"Even Joel," she said.

"When?" Ralphy asked. He was walking around in tight circles, something he often did when he was nervous or excited or both.

"What movie star?" I asked. "What film is he shooting?"

Lisa grinned. "Any more questions?"

"Plenty," Mike said.

We asked.

And she gave us all the answers we needed.

CHAPTER 4

Just over one week later, all five of us sat in a weather machine as it began to fall out of the sky.

That's the way my dad describes it when he is trying to be funny with the kind of dumb humor that grown-ups use far too often. He likes to argue that jets are weather machines. There's one kind of weather around it when you step inside, and there's different weather around it when you step outside a few hours later. Like the time that we went from the airport near Jamesville to Hawaii. And he also likes to argue that when a jet lands, it's nothing more than the controlled fall of an object weighing a couple hundred tons and moving hundreds of miles an hour.

The worst of it was that his humor was rubbing off on me.

"Nice weather machine, huh?" I had said to Mike as we made ourselves comfortable at the beginning of the trip. Lisa and Ralphy and Joel were in a row behind us.

Mike had looked at me like I was crazy, so I'd

explained that when we got out of the plane next, we'd be stepping into different weather. He had just sighed, rolled his eyeballs, and went back to reading his comic book.

And now, as the pilot announced we would be on the ground in twenty minutes, I was dumb enough to repeat my mistake.

"We're falling," I told Mike.

He had ignored the pilot and was half snoozing, and my comment made him bolt into an upright position, his mouth half open with panic.

"What!"

"A couple hundred tons of metal," I said. "Dropping from thirty thousand feet at hundreds of miles an hour. I'd call that falling. Wouldn't you?"

"You're such a meatball," he said. He must have still been angry that he'd lost the coin toss for the window seat. There was a really large woman on the other side of him, and she was taking up half of his middle seat. Plus it smelled like she didn't believe in deodorant. Or showers. Me, I had a window and the clear blue sky.

"Meatball?" I said. "That hurt. I've got feelings, you know."

"Hide them. I'm not interested. And lean back so I can catch the view."

I did.

Below us were mountains, looking like folded ridges of crumpled olive-green paper. An hour earlier, we'd crossed over the Grand Canyon. Then stretches of desert. And now the mountains, growing larger as the plane slowly descended. Minutes later, we saw the valley of the Los

Angeles basin, and the endless square miles of buildings. We came in from the north, and the ocean was to our right. I saw a few large islands and the dots of ships on the water.

"Welcome to La-la land," Mike said, leaning across me as he peered through my window.

"La-la land?"

"It's another name for Los Angeles," he explained. "Because sometimes it's called L.A., and because all the time it's la-la crazy. Get it? La-la land."

Mike whipped out a pair of dark sunglasses and perched them on his nose. "What do you think, dude? Do I look like I belong on a surfboard?"

"Mike?"

"Yeah?"

"You're such a meatball."

A chauffeur was waiting for us at the luggage carrousel. We knew he was there for us because he held a big sign with letters handwritten in black felt marker: HIGGINS PARTY.

"That's us," Lisa said, waving at the big man. He had tanned skin, dark hair, a bleached blond goatee, and was wearing a blue uniform.

"Cool," he said. "I'm Vince. I'll get some help for your luggage."

And it was that easy. Another guy loaded all our suit-cases onto a giant cart and wheeled it out to a long black limousine with smoked-glass windows. All of us stepped from ninety-degree heat into the air-conditioned leather interior.

"Wow!" Ralphy said.

It seemed bigger than the inside of a bus.

We made ourselves comfortable.

"Wow!" Mike said. "A television. Turn it on, Lisa!"

"A mini-fridge," Ralphy said. "Grab us some sodas, Joel!"

So this was the lifestyle of the rich and famous. Limousines, chauffeurs, and beverages and television as we traveled down the freeways of Southern California. I figured I could get used to it.

Movement outside my window caught my eye. Two large men had moved up beside Vince, our chauffeur, one on each side. They grabbed Vince by the elbows and moved him down the sidewalk toward a van with an open side door. They shoved him inside and the van sped away.

"Guys . . ." I said. "Something funny is going on here."

"Yeah," Mike said. "*I Love Lucy* reruns."

Laughter came from the television.

"No," I said. "Not ha-ha funny but strange funny. Our chauffeur was just—"

The driver's door opened and shut. One of the two large men who had shoved Vince inside the van slid behind the steering wheel. The other large man got in the passenger side.

And our limousine eased forward into traffic.

"Relax," Mike said. He had on his dark sunglasses again. He was leaning back, hands behind his head, elbows high, feet propped on the opposite seat. "Dude, so we have a different driver. What's the big deal?"

He turned to Joel. "Could you find a slice of lemon in the fridge and squeeze it into an iced soda for me?"

"Duuuude," Joel said. He sat with a tattered teddy bear beside him, his equivalent to a comfort blanket. Seeing my little brother with his tousled brown hair and his sweet, innocent grin and his attempt to imitate a California surfer dude made my heart lurch with fear. *What if something happens to him?*

"Mike, I'm serious." I kept my voice low. "Two guys threw our driver, Vince, into a van. The van drove off. The two guys got in this car. Now they're driving us somewhere."

"I'm sure Jericho Stone set it up this way," Mike said.

"I'm not."

The car stopped at a light. I wondered if it would be smart to jump out now, wave down traffic, and get a police cruiser to pull the limo over and rescue everyone. I pulled on the door handle to check whether it would open.

Nothing.

The doors were locked.

I tried unlocking the door, but the locks didn't move.

And the limousine shot forward.

"Nuts." I fell back in my seat. "This isn't good."

"Relax," Mike said. "Oh, Joel, not too much lemon, please."

Joel handed him a soda.

"You look really worried," Lisa said to me.

"You guys didn't see them pull Vince away?"

She shook her head. "Why don't you ask them about it?"

I moved forward. There was dark glass between the passenger compartment and the front of the limo. I slid it open.

"Hello," I said. "Could you—"

"Shut the glass," the driver growled without turning his head. "Shut up. Sit back. And don't try to get out of the car again. If you do get out, your friends are going to get hurt really bad without you. But if you keep cool, you'll be fine. Just think of this as a free sight-seeing tour. Got it?"

"But, but—"

"Shut the glass, Richard. Between the two of us, we outweigh you by four hundred pounds. You don't want to make us angry."

I shut the glass.

I turned back to the others.

They all stared at me, their mouths open.

So they'd heard.

"I don't get it," Lisa said. "We're being kidnapped?"

"La-la land," Mike said bitterly. "We pick the one limousine that gets carjacked. What are the odds of that?"

By then, I had moved to the back of the limo so I could talk to them quietly.

"I don't think this was random bad luck," I told Mike.

Outside the limo, palm trees slid by, their long, jagged leaves outlined against the sky. We were traveling down a boulevard, with masses of cars and taxis and trucks surrounding us.

"Not an accident?"

"He called me Richard," I answered.

"They were waiting for us?" Ralphy said. "Why? It's not like we're rich or we have rich parents. Why would anyone want to kidnap us?"

The limo slowed to make a turn. I hoped for another light. Maybe all five of us could somehow get the doors open and jump out.

I saw a sign that said 405. The limo picked up speed again.

"We're going onto the freeway," I said. "Ralphy, remember that map you tried boring us with for the last three days? Tell me it's not in your suitcase."

"My laptop bag," he said, pointing. It was at his feet.

"Good. We need to know exactly where we are headed."

"How's that going to help?" Mike asked.

"I'm not sure," I said. "But it's not going to hurt. And it

looks like all we can do is sit back here and wait to see where they take us."

What I didn't say out loud were the rest of my thoughts.

Where they take us matters a lot less than what they intend to do with us once we get there.

CHAPTER 6

Lisa ignored most of our conversation as Mike and Ralphy and I tried to read the map of Los Angeles. We were on Interstate 405, going south, away from the airport. The traffic was six lanes wide in each direction, and the limo moved at a steady pace, not too slow, not too fast.

"Here," I said to Ralphy. I noticed a sign for an exit on the side of the highway and matched it to one on the map. "We're right here."

"Not good," Ralphy said. "We're going the opposite direction of Hollywood."

He stabbed his finger on the map, showing a place north of the airport. Where we were supposed to meet the actor named Jericho Stone.

"I still want to believe this is some kind of thing that Stone has set up," Mike said.

"Why would he do that?" I asked.

"Hidden cameras in the limo, recording our reaction." Mike began to search for the cameras. "So let's act cool, like this isn't a big deal."

"Or maybe we can hold up this sign," Lisa said.

She showed us what she'd been working on that had kept her quiet. A piece of paper with these words written in block letters: CALL POLICE. WE HAVE BEEN ABDUCTED.

She pushed the paper against the window beside her, then groaned.

"Smoked-glass windows," she said. "No one can see this."

"You sure?" Mike stuck his face against the window and made faces at passing drivers. He didn't get any reactions. "I guess you're right."

"Hold one side," Lisa told me. "I'll hold the other. When Ralphy lowers the window, we'll make sure it doesn't get blown away."

I took an edge of the paper and nodded at Ralphy. He tried one of the power buttons.

"Window won't lower," he said. "They must have locked it from up front."

Mike sighed. "This is exactly why I'd like to have my own cell phone."

I agreed. A cell phone would have been handy. But we didn't have one, and it looked like we were stuck until they stopped.

The ride lasted for at least another hour. We knew exactly where we were on the map, but I didn't think the knowledge would do us much good. The limo had taken us south on 405 to a major east-west interstate, then east for a half hour, then turned off on a smaller highway, and from there through an area of large houses as the road wound up a mountain, and then beyond the houses, over the mountain, and miles down the other side.

"This doesn't look good," Ralphy said. He was sitting on his hands, rocking back and forth.

"Are you kidding?" Mike said. "It looks great. Rugged hills, deep canyons, shrubs, bushes, blue sky. A beautiful place for a picnic."

That told me Mike was scared, too. I knew him well enough to know that making jokes was what he did when he didn't want people to guess his true feelings.

The limo turned off the pavement and followed a dirt road until it reached a gate that swung open automatically. As the limo moved through, the gate shut behind us.

"Now what?" Lisa whispered.

I didn't have an answer. It was obvious that the limo couldn't go much farther. I didn't want to think about what was waiting for us at the end.

The limo climbed another hill, and at the top, where it flattened, we saw a small helicopter, its blades turning and throwing dust. The loudness of the engine reached us clearly inside the limo.

"If they take us away in that," Ralphy said in a trembling voice, "we could end up hundreds of miles from here."

"I just don't get it," Lisa said. "Why us? What does it gain them?"

Before any of us could try to answer her, the driver of the limo slammed on the brakes and spun the car around. As the limo stopped, both men dashed out of the limo, slamming the front doors as they ran away.

"Huh?" Mike said.

I kept my eyes on both men. They ran directly to the helicopter. Someone inside—it looked like a woman—flung open a door, and both large men jumped inside. The door shut behind them. Seconds later the helicopter rose from the ground, tilted forward, and made a graceful turn as it headed away from us.

"Huh?" Mike said again. "That's it? We're alone?"

I tried the rear door of the limo, and this time it opened. I stepped outside. Dry heat surrounded me as I stretched.

"We're alone," I said. The chugging sound of the helicopter engine was fading as the helicopter disappeared around a far hill.

Mike and Ralphy joined me outside. The buzzing of insects and the lack of breeze and the clear blue of the sky made it seem very peaceful.

"Now I'm really confused," Mike said. "They kidnap us and then leave us by ourselves?"

"We can walk back," Ralphy said. "All we need to do is follow the road that we came in on."

"Maybe it's a trap," I said. This didn't make any sense at all. There was nothing for anyone to gain by kidnapping us. But why go to all the work and risk and then let us go?

Mike opened the driver's door. "They took the keys. I was kind of hoping I could try to drive us back."

"We want to live," Ralphy said. "Let's stick to walking. We'll take bottles of water and soda from the limo's fridge and we'll be fine."

"And noise will give plenty of notice if the helicopter

comes back," Lisa said. "All we would need to do is hide under some bushes."

"Snakes," Ralphy said. "As long as we don't see snakes."

"'Fraidy cat," Mike said. "There's nothing out here that can hurt us."

Just as he finished saying that, a loud roar filled the air.

Mike laughed nervously. "Boy, if we were in Africa, I'd bet anyone that was a lion. But that's crazy. We're not in Africa. Right?"

As if in answer to his question, the roar grew louder. And closer.

Fifty yards away, at the edge of the clearing, the bushes moved.

Out stepped a large male lion. Followed by two females. And all three started padding across the grass toward us.

CHAPTER 7

"Let's not panic," I said in a low voice, "This would be a good time to slowly get back in the limo."

But I was speaking to air.

Mike and Ralphy had already dived back into the limo with Joel and Lisa.

The lions began to sprint toward me.

I ignored my own advice.

I panicked. And was anything but slow as I jumped through the door that Mike held open for me from inside the limo.

He slammed it shut just as the male lion reached the side of the car.

It sniffed at the windows, its massive head swinging from side to side. Its large whiskers seemed like spikes sticking out the sides of its mouth.

"Wow," I said, leaning back even though the window protected me from the lion. "That was close."

The two females joined the male. They prowled

around the limo for a few minutes and finally settled down beside the car. They were so close that I could have reached out the window and leaned down and tickled their manes. If I were crazy enough to want to lose my arm.

"I don't get it," Mike said. "Lions? Here in Southern California? That's impossible."

"You're right," I said. "Totally impossible. They don't exist. So go back out there and pretend they are a figment of your imagination."

"Maybe this is some sort of game preserve," Lisa said. "Remember the gate on our way in?"

"None of this makes any sense at all," I said. "We get kidnapped from the airport. Driven into a game preserve. Our drivers race into a helicopter and leave us here. Why? Why? Why?"

Joel had taken out a disposable camera. He was clicking pictures of the lions, as if this was the coolest thing he could have asked for on his first day in Southern California.

"The question isn't why," Mike said. "It's what do we do next?"

"Nothing," I answered. "We're safe here inside the limo."

"At least we have that going for us," Mike said. "Unless the lions can figure out how to open doors."

"I don't know," Ralphy said in a miserable voice. "I think I'm in trouble."

Mike leaned over and shut the door locks. "That make you feel better?"

"No," he said.

"It's okay, Ralphy," Lisa said. "Like Ricky said, as long as we stay inside the limo, we're fine."

"That's just it." Ralphy's voice lost none of its misery. "I need to get out."

"What?" Mike said. "Are you nuts?"

Ralphy shook his head. "Remember all the free sodas in the fridge?"

We nodded.

"I think I drank too many of them." Ralphy crossed his legs and squeezed hard. His face showed agony. "I don't know how much longer I can wait."

"How much water do you think flows over Niagara Falls every second?" Mike asked me a few minutes later. "I mean, think of it. All that water gushing, gushing, gushing. Sploosh, sploosh, sploosh. Like the world's biggest faucet, draining all that water."

Ralphy moaned.

"Mike, that's cruel," I said. "Ralphy doesn't want to hear about water right now. Right, Ralphy?"

Ralphy was leaning over. He lifted his head long enough to agree with me.

"Nor does he want to hear about garden hoses when you turn on the faucet," I said. "Right, Ralphy? Or about the gurgling sound when you pour water out of a bottle. Right, Ralphy?"

"Shhh!" Lisa said.

"Hey," Mike said. "Don't you remember when Ralphy

put Tabasco sauce in a water pistol and squirted it up my nose? I think now's a great time to talk about a waterfall."

"It was an accident," Ralphy said. "Really."

"Shhhh!" Lisa said.

"It was," Ralphy said. "I had it loaded because I was afraid of the neighbor's German shepherd, and I got the water pistols mixed up and—"

"Shhhh!" Lisa said. "Listen!"

"Don't be bossy," Mike said. "We don't have to listen if we—"

"No!" Lisa pointed upward. "I mean listen outside."

We listened.

"A helicopter," I said. "Those guys are coming back!"

"We're protected by lions now," Mike said. He grinned. "And if they get really nasty, Ralphy can always wet himself inside the helicopter."

"Hah, hah," Ralphy said.

The helicopter grew louder.

Its shadow fell across the lions. They got up and stretched. Still the helicopter hovered. It was so loud that none of us in the limo could have heard anything we said to one another.

A minute later a white pickup truck drove up toward the limo, with a gray-bearded man behind the steering wheel. The truck had a logo on the side door that that read *Jones, Animal Trainer*. Behind it was a cage on a small trailer bed.

He roared to a stop beside us and stepped out with a long stick and waved his arms at the lions. They ran to the back of the trailer. The gray-bearded man stepped beside them and opened the doors to the cage on top of the trailer.

He prodded the lions with his long stick, and when they jumped into the giant cage he shut the doors.

The man stepped away from the truck and impatiently pointed at the helicopter and then pointed at the ground. He got in the truck and backed up, giving the helicopter room to land.

"So much for the lions giving us protection," I yelled at Mike.

As it turned out, it didn't matter that the lions were gone.

Because when the helicopter landed and the engine shut down, one of Hollywood's most famous action stars stepped out and toward our limo.

Jericho Stone. Tall. Dark hair. Chiseled face. A man that millions had seen and adored in smash-hit movies all across the world. The guy who had invited us here to Hollywood. Who had arranged the limo to pick us up at the airport.

With the lions locked up, Ralphy bolted out of the limo.

Jericho smiled his famous smile, moved toward Ralphy, and stuck out a hand in greeting.

"Out of the way!" Ralphy shouted. Ralphy pushed him aside and kept running until he disappeared into the bushes on the far side of the clearing.

Jericho gave a puzzled shrug and stepped toward us as we left the limo.

"Good day, Mr. Stone," Lisa said. "We're glad to see you."

"I'm glad to see you guys," he said. "I recognize Mike and Ricky from the video clip. And that was Ralphy, right, the guy who ran away? So you must be Lisa. And the younger one must be Joel."

Lisa nodded.

"Sorry about the mix-up," Jericho Stone said.

"Mix-up?" Mike echoed. "This was a mix-up?"

Jericho ignored the question and waved for the gray-bearded man to join us.

Up close, the man wasn't as old as he'd first appeared. He wore a black T-shirt and blue jeans and cowboy boots. His muscular body stretched the T-shirt, and his forearms seemed as large as Popeye's.

"Maverick Jones," he said, introducing himself. "Just call me Mav. I'm an animal trainer."

We introduced ourselves to him.

"Mr. Stone . . ." I said.

"Call me Jericho. If we're going to spend a week together, I'll get real tired of being called 'Mister.'"

"Jericho," I said. "What did you mean by calling this a mix-up? And how did you know how to find us here?"

Before he could answer, Ralphy screamed again. There was a loud crashing of bushes, and he headed straight our way, with a female lion lazily trotting in pursuit.

"Aaaagh!" Ralphy screamed. "Aaaagh!"

"That explains where Lucy was," Mav Jones said. "She always likes to play with the guests."

Ralphy ran past us, still screaming. Lucy the lion stayed close behind.

"Yup," Mav said. He had a toothpick in his mouth, and

he moved it around before speaking again. "Soon as he slows down, she'll lose interest. 'Course, the way he's going, he might reach the bears in a couple of minutes. That ought to scare him right back this direction again."

CHAPTER 8

Overlooking a swimming pool that overlooked the Hollywood Hills that overlooked the skyscrapers of downtown Los Angeles was much better than being stuck in a limo with lions outside.

I said as much to Mike and Ralphy.

"No kidding," Ralphy said. "And suntanning with music in the background sure beats being chased by those lions."

On the game preserve a couple hours earlier, it had taken a few minutes in the truck to catch up to Ralphy. By then, he'd tired enough to slow down to a fast walk, and his yelling had dropped to mere moans. Lucy the lion had been content to keep pace like a friendly dog. After calming Ralphy, we'd all flown in the helicopter to a landing pad in the nearby hills of Hollywood, where a car and driver waited for us, and then Jericho had helped us settle into his house, showing each of us to our own rooms. He had introduced us to Erika, the nanny he had hired for the week as part of the agreement he'd made with Lisa's parents when he'd invited us to

Hollywood.

His house wasn't exactly like any house in our small town of Jamesville. It was set into the side of a hill, with part of the house on giant stilts that Jericho assured us were strong enough to withstand any earthquake. The house—actually, mansion—had marbled floors and high ceilings and huge picture windows that overlooked the valley. It didn't have much of a backyard, just hedges and plants around a swimming pool lined with thick, padded lawn chairs and patio sets with umbrellas.

Jericho had left us at the pool, telling us he needed to go consult with his director back at the location of the movie that he was shooting. The movie was being filmed at a place nearby called Griffin Park, where there was a zoo, a couple of golf courses, riding trails for horses, and a couple of museums.

So now we were basking at the pool, listening to a radio station that played oldies from the '70s and '80s, and suntanning.

"Another soda?" Mike asked Ralphy. "Probably won't be any more lions around to chase you out of the bushes."

"Very, very funny," Ralphy said. "You would have run, too. How was I to know that the lions belonged to Mav Jones and that he's the animal trainer for the movie that Jericho is shooting?"

"Maybe because all of the lions were really old and had had their fangs and claws removed?" Mike said.

Which was true. Mav supplied animals for movie shoots, and many of them just *looked* dangerous.

"Let me remind you," I told Mike, "when *you* first saw

them, you jumped in the limo faster than Superman."

"Just so Lisa and Joel would feel better about being afraid," he said.

"You know," Lisa said from her lawn chair, "I guess it makes some sort of sense that Jericho would know Mav Jones because Jones is supplying animals for the movie that Jericho's working on right now. But what do you think about the rest of it?"

"You mean the part about the limo drivers getting mixed up?" I asked.

"Exactly," she said. "Like it was no big deal that it seemed like we'd been kidnapped."

After arriving by helicopter at the wild animal preserve, Jericho Stone had said that the drivers thought they were supposed to bring us to the Jones training grounds because that's where Jericho was going to be. And Jericho had said they must have been mixed up because he did indeed have a meeting with Mav Jones at that time, and Jericho's secretary must have given them the wrong place by accident.

"Well," I said, "it didn't seem like Jericho and Mav had much to talk about when Jericho got there, so I wonder if they actually did have a meeting."

"Come on," Mike said. "Once Jericho saw we were there, he wouldn't have had time for a meeting. They probably re-scheduled it for some other time."

"But why did the drivers throw Vince in a van and steal the limo?" I asked.

"Your imagination?" Mike said. "You're the only one who saw it. And Stone told us that Vince called him an hour later and said everything was fine."

"But you heard them threaten me, right?"

Silence. They couldn't disagree with me.

"So," I said. "Either it was a mix-up and Jericho is telling the truth, weird as it seems that the drivers of the limo would leave us by helicopter. Or we were kidnapped and Jericho is lying about it. Why?"

"Doesn't want bad publicity," Lisa suggested.

"But if we really were kidnapped," Ralphy said, "how did Jericho know where to find us? I mean, why would kidnappers go to all that trouble and then not only let us go but tell Jericho *where* they'd let us go? Remember, Stone told us that his secretary called immediately after the mix-up, and she told him where to find us. So if she knew where to find us, how could it have been a kidnapping?"

"And that brings us to the original question. Why would we be kidnapped in the first place?"

Again, silence, except for the radio in the background.

"I say let's enjoy the sunshine and the view," Mike said a few minutes later. "We're here safe. We're in Hollywood. And tomorrow we're going to learn about the movie business with a famous actor. So what else should we worry about?"

We all agreed with him.

As it turned out, we should have worried plenty more.

CHAPTER 9

"Everybody ready?"

It was the following morning. We sat in a rented van, and all of us answered Erika's question with enthusiasm. She was a tall, blond woman about my mom's age, and she'd treated us like her own children. She'd cooked us a great breakfast of ham and eggs and pancakes, expressing amazement at how much Mike and Ralphy and I ate. She'd helped us get ready after that, making sure we weren't late for the 7:30 A.M. departure in the van. And now she was driving us to the movie location in Griffin Park. Jericho had not returned until late the night before, and he had left again at 5:30 A.M. to get to the set in time for makeup. Erika, in short, was the one who would be looking out for us all week.

"Good," she said. "You guys will really enjoy this."

With that, she drove out the narrow, twisting driveway of Jericho's mansion. At the gate, she stopped and pressed a button on a remote control for it to swing open. She pulled out slowly onto a street called Mulholland Drive.

"Too cool," Mike said as the van picked up speed. "Way too cool."

He was right. We passed huge Mediterranean-style mansions with locked gates. The hills—actually called the Santa Monica Mountains, as Ralphy had pointed out—were etched against blue sky. There was a slight haze in the valley. I'd wondered if it was smog, but Erika had said it was too early in the day. The haze was known as a marine layer, a type of mist that drifted in from the ocean and hung over the city until the sun burned it away.

We stared at the mansions and the views as Mulholland Drive wound along the top of the Santa Monica Mountains. Occasionally we'd have a good view of the San Fernando Valley to the north and then, minutes later, an equally good view of Los Angeles to the south.

Joel, of course, kept snapping photos. He was on his third disposable camera already. Ten of his shots had been of Ralphy running at full speed from Lucy; I could hardly wait for those to be developed.

"Look!" Lisa said. "Universal City!"

Sure enough, it was on the north side of the mountains. And on our schedule to visit sometime during the week.

"Great place," Erika said. From where I sat in the backseat, I could see her smile in the rearview mirror. "Of course, it won't be nearly as exciting as being on an actual movie set, though. Tell me again why Jericho Stone invited you."

We let Lisa explain. She told Erika that after we'd shot the anti-drug video, Lisa had sent a copy of it by e-mail to her older brother, Jonathan, who lived in Chicago and worked for an advertising agency, to ask him if he thought it was good. He'd loved it and, without telling Lisa, had e-mailed it to one of his former college roommates, named Eldon Eldridge, who loved it, too, and who sent an e-mail back to Jonathan asking if the kids who'd produced it would like to see what it was like on a real movie set. Because for Eldon, money didn't really matter that much. He could easily afford to fly all of us to Los Angeles and to hire a nanny to look after us for the week. That's because Eldon Eldridge had stopped using his real name just after graduating college and had gone to a stage name as he pursued acting. And that stage name, of course, was Jericho Stone.

And that's why we were here.

When Lisa finished telling the story, Erika applauded.

"That's just great," she said. "Someone should be filming you guys here. It'd be a great publicity thing. Famous movie star supports kids who produce anti-drug video."

"Sure," Mike said. "I mean, look at my profile. Is this the kind of face that looks good on film or what?"

Lisa, sitting on the other side of Mike, elbowed him. "Jericho Stone's not in it for the publicity," she told Erika. "He's one of my brother's best friends and thought it would be nice to let us see the movie business up close."

"We could show you the video," Ralphy said.

"No thanks," Erika said, laughing again. "Too gross for me."

"You've seen it?" Lisa asked.

Erika shook her head. "What I meant to say was it's *probably* too gross for me. I mean, if guys like this made it..."

Lisa nodded. "You should have heard some of their ideas."

"Hey," Erika said, pointing out the window. "There's part of Warner Brothers Studios."

We were on a road at the base of the hills now. Warner Bros. Studios was to our left, with the olive-colored bush of the hillside to our right.

We passed a cemetery stretching up the hill.

"Forest Lawn Cemetery," Erika said. "A lot of famous movie stars are buried there. And up ahead is our turn to Griffin Park, where they're shooting the scenes at the zoo today. You guys will have an exciting day."

And she was right.

But not, perhaps, in the way she'd intended.

CHAPTER 10

The real excitement started with an explosion.

Before that, however, Jericho Stone had invited us to his trailer. It was on the movie set, which was tucked away in the back part of the Griffin Park zoo. Because the zoo was so huge, not even the movie producer was able to get zoo officials to shut it down entirely. Instead, a portion of the zoo had been roped off to the public, well guarded by security people who checked the badges of everyone going into the movie set area.

Stone's trailer was far from the security ropes and well away from any view of the public. Erika drove us to a specially marked area of the zoo parking lot and showed her parking pass to security. From there, she took us through the zoo entrance, past the monkey cages, past the giraffe enclosure, and toward the big cats. There, more security officials checked all our badges and pointed us in the direction of Stone's trailer.

We walked past small crowds of people who milled around cameramen and set workers, and we found the trailer overlooking the lion pit. Jericho answered the knock on his door, and Erika waved good-bye and wished us luck one more time. Then she left.

"Guys," Jericho said, with the warm grin that made women all across the nation swoon, "come on in."

I still found it hard to believe that he seemed like such a regular guy.

Of course, regular guys didn't have luxury air-conditioned trailers parked in the middle of a movie set. Or leather recliners and big color televisions and fully equipped kitchens in their trailers.

"Make yourselves comfortable," he said. "I've got about ten minutes before I need to go on the set."

Ralphy went straight to the fridge and found a soda. A person would think he'd have learned from the day before, but he cracked it open and began to drink.

Stone noticed that I was staring at a simple silver cross hung on the wall.

"I keep that there as a reminder," Stone said. "In college, Lisa's brother, Jonathan seemed to have such a balanced and peaceful life that I listened closely whenever he talked about his faith. When I became a believer, it gave me so much. In this industry especially, when it's too easy to get hung up on money and power."

"Cool," Mike said.

"Actually, it is," Stone said. "Spirituality is such a major part of being human that it's very cool to search and find the answers to why and how we have a soul. I'm in a position where I can show that to a lot of people I work with."

I tried to ignore a mean thought. *If Jericho Stone really is who he says he is, why does it seem like he hasn't been completely honest about yesterday's events?* I was very sure we'd been kidnapped, but he acted like we hadn't.

I tried to ignore another mean thought. That's what he was. An actor. *Is he acting now in telling us about his faith?*

I hid those thoughts.

Stone held up some papers. "The script. Just reading through today's scenes."

We knew the name of the movie because it was on our security passes. *Shroud of the Lion.* But we didn't know much else about it.

Stone anticipated our question. "It's about two guys who steal a huge diamond from a mine in Africa. They smuggle it into the States in a lion that is flown here for an animal trainer who is in on the deal. Except the lion gets mixed up with another one that is being delivered to the zoo."

"Smuggled it *in* a lion?" I asked. I had a vision of the guy sticking his arm all the way down a lion's throat to plant a diamond there.

Jericho laughed. "They feed it to the lion in a hunk of meat. Expecting it will come out a couple of days later."

"Come out?" Mike asked.

"You know," Stone said. "In one end and out the other. . . ."

"Yuck!" Lisa made a face.

"Exactly," Stone said. "So the bad guys get themselves hired at the zoo, where they start looking for the diamond."

"You mean . . ." Ralphy said.

Stone laughed again. "Let me put it this way. If you went

to the lion pit right now, you'd see a lot of places to look. Giant kitty droppings."

"Gross!" Lisa said.

"Exactly," Jericho said. "Think about it. Two bad guys pretending to be animal vets. They get put into crazy situations as they get called to fix the other animals. At the same time, they have to dodge the lions as they try to find time to get in and out of the lion pit and steal the lion droppings to look for a diamond. It comes in a lot bigger package than what house cats leave behind. And they have to go through dozens of piles hoping to find it."

"Gross!" Lisa said again.

Stone nodded. "Gross sells. In Hollywood, people think of concepts. So this one is kind of like *Ace Ventura* meets *Dumb and Dumber*. I play the good guy, a cop who is on the trail of the diamond."

"That's why," I said, thinking of the day before, "a real-life animal trainer is involved with this movie."

"Mav Jones." Stone nodded. "We're using his lions as stand-ins for the lions here. I don't want to spend any time in the lion pit with the zoo lions. We keep a rifle with knock-out darts for when we're working with the bigger animals, like giraffes. But we won't use the zoo's lions. They have teeth and claws, and they don't really like people except as possible food."

"So," I said, "it's a movie about a crooked animal trainer, and to shoot the movie you need a real animal trainer."

"Yup. Hollywood irony, huh. Mav even gets a stand-in part. He's excited about that."

Stone patted the script. "I can get you guys a copy if you

want. I know you'll only be standing in as extras, but you might like to see how the movie is shot from script."

We all nodded.

Stone settled back in his comfy chair. "What I want to know from you guys is how you shot your anti-drug video. Ricky, hold up your right hand."

I did.

"All your fingers. On the video, it looked like every one had been smashed into burritos. How did you do it?"

"Mike's idea," I said. "He—"

Boom!

An explosion rocked the back end of the trailer.

Instantly, a cloud of black smoke began to mushroom toward us.

CHAPTER 11

At the back end of the trailer—near the home entertainment center—flames shot up from the carpeting. The oily black smoke curled into the air like angry snakes.

"Out! Out! Out!" Jericho said. "This is not a drill!"

Those were instructions he did not have to repeat. Mike reached the door first and kicked it open. He waited at the top of the steps, pulling Lisa out and pushing her down. Ralphy followed. I grabbed Joel and shoved him forward. Mike helped him, too. Then I ran and cleared the entire steps by jumping out of the trailer.

I landed hard, almost smacking my chin on my knees as my legs took the impact. But I didn't fall over. I caught my balance and looked back for Jericho.

He was not to be seen!

By now dozens of people had gathered around the trailer.

"He's in there!" I shouted and pointed at the

trailer. Black smoke poured from the open door.

No one seemed to understand.

I covered my mouth with my hand and jumped back up the steps.

"Jericho!"

No answer.

I tried looking inside. The smoke attacked my eyes. I dropped to my knees.

"Jericho!"

Out of the smoke, a pair of blue-jeaned legs appeared.

"Go!" he shouted. "Go!"

He followed as I turned.

A blast of foam hit us.

I gagged and spit and gasped for air.

I fell down the steps.

It took me a second to realize what had happened. Fire fighters. Four of them. Blasting from extinguishers. Later I would find out they were part of a group of safety experts on the set for possible danger from some of the stunts with explosives.

All I knew then was that they were wading forward into the smoke, masks on, blowing white spray to fight the fire.

Someone hauled me to my feet and doused me with water to get rid of the foam.

"You okay, kid?"

I sputtered out an answer.

I heard shouts beside me.

Two other people were trying to drag Jericho away as he fought them.

"I'm all right, I'm all right!" he said.

They ignored him.

As he struggled, something fell from his hands.

He tried to stop to pick it up, but his rescuers kept dragging him away.

With all the attention on the star of the movie, the person who had picked me up let me go. I was closest to the object, and, to help Jericho, I retrieved it.

I was ignored by all the onlookers. Their attention was on the trailer and the fire and the fire fighters or on the sight of Jericho Stone being dragged away by two of the other safety experts.

With the back of one hand, I wiped my forehead to stop the water dripping into my eyes. With my other hand, I brought the object up to study it.

It was about the size of a cell phone, with a computer-like screen that filled half of its face. The screen was blank, and there were only six buttons, none of them with numbers like the keypad of a regular cell phone.

What is it?

I realized that it had been important enough for Jericho to risk his life. He had not followed us out of the trailer but had stayed inside to find it.

But why? What was it for?

As I stared at it, the screen blinked into life. It beeped twice, and then a small star appeared all alone in the center of the screen.

Around it, lines and tiny numbers grew into focus.

I stared at it. Suddenly it made sense.

A map!

A map of the roads around the zoo.

And the star at the center began to move.

I spun to show it to Mike and Ralphy and Lisa.

At that moment, a pair of hands gripped my shoulders.

"Let's get you to a doctor, son."

"But . . . but . . ."

I had no choice. Those strong hands propelled me forward. I didn't even get the chance to see who was pushing me away from the crowd.

Onlookers stepped aside as the man behind me kept shoving me forward.

And once I was past them, the hands left my shoulders and grabbed the cell phone–like thing from my fingers.

"Hey!" I said.

But it was too late.

The man had already started to run away from me.

CHAPTER 12

"You're telling me," Mike said, "that the guy who dragged you away from Stone's trailer was the driver of the limo?"

"Not Vince, the original driver," I said. "The driver who kidnapped us. If it was a kidnapping."

Mike and Ralphy and I were walking through the zoo. Half an hour had passed since the fire at the trailer. Long enough for the excitement to die down. Jericho Stone had made sure all of us were all right, then had excused himself for another production meeting.

"The limo driver," Ralphy echoed. We stopped in front of a monkey cage, where Mike immediately began scratching under his arms and making *ooohoooh aaaah-aaaah* noises.

"I think," I said, "that the guy was more interested in taking away the computer device than in me."

A Japanese tourist nearby turned his video camera away from the monkey cage and began to film Mike's bad imitation of a monkey. I didn't inform

Mike that he was on camera; when this vacation shot got back to Japan, somebody was going to find him amusing.

"Tell me about the handheld," Ralphy said, immediately much more interested now that I'd mentioned anything to do with computers.

I described it.

"Sounds like some kind of PDA," Ralphy said. "Maybe a Palm Pilot."

Mike stopped making his monkey noises. "I've got a Palm Pilot for all my notes," Mike said. He took a pen from Ralphy's front pocket and began to jot something on the palm of his left hand. "Note to self: Zoo keepers think Ricky and Ralphy are escaped monkeys."

Mike held up his left hand so we could see the jottings on the palm. "See? My Palm Pilot."

"You're a riot," I told Mike. "Get back to your monkey imitations. I think the female in the cage here has fallen in love with you."

I turned to Ralphy. "PDA?"

"Personal Data Assistant. Exactly as you described it. A miniature computer."

"But the markings on the screen. Like it was a map. And the crazy little numbers at the bottom."

"Numbers?" Ralphy squinted. Not because of the strong sunshine across his face, but because he always squinted like that when faced with a computer problem.

I closed my eyes to picture the small screen and those numbers. I read them back to Ralphy from my memory.

"If I didn't know better," Ralphy said, "I'd say those are coordinates. Latitude and longitude. And you said a little star was moving inside the map on the screen."

I nodded.

"Here's my guess, then." Ralphy's face lost its squint. "The PDA was a locator device. Able to track movement of something."

"Huh?" This came from Mike, who paused in his efforts to get the monkeys in front of him to scratch under their arms.

"Sure," Ralphy said, warming up to his subject. "Like if an electronic beeper was hidden on a car. The PDA can track the car's movements."

"That's CIA stuff," Mike said.

"Maybe ten years ago," Ralphy answered. "You wouldn't believe the stuff you can get on the Internet now. Tracking devices, mini-spy cameras, equipment for listening in on conversations . . ."

Mike didn't disagree. When it came to stuff like this, Ralphy was rarely wrong.

"So let me get this straight, then. In order for your theory to be correct, that means Jericho is or was trying to keep track of something or someone. But someone else knew about it and wanted to steal his tracking device. So they set his trailer on fire to get it."

"Or maybe to destroy it, and they were surprised when he stayed in to get it," Ralphy said. "But that person would have to know a lot about Jericho."

"And be watching from nearby," I added. "Just like it happened."

"And," Ralphy said, "that doesn't even answer why Jericho is trying to keep track of something, whatever it was."

"And . . ." Mike held up his forefinger like a lecturing professor.

Ralphy and I waited.

". . . and it means that whatever Jericho was trying to track got away from him."

"And the limo driver who kidnapped us and stole the PDA from me—"

"If it really was a kidnapping," Ralphy interrupted.

"If we really were kidnapped, the limo driver now knows where to find whatever it was that Jericho was trying to track."

"There's got to be a simpler explanation," Mike said. "Why in the world would a guy like Jericho Stone have a secret this complicated?"

I stared at Mike thoughtfully. "Good question, pal. Maybe we should start there."

"Oh no," he said. "I'm just here on a vacation. I'm just here to be an extra in a movie. I'm just here for sunshine and ice-cream cones. In fact, I'm going to go looking for an ice-cream cone right now."

Mike walked away from us.

I looked at Ralphy. "Are you just here for sunshine and ice cream? After all, how much could it hurt to try to learn a little more?"

Stupid question, I would tell myself later. Very stupid question.

CHAPTER  13

"Pieces of chalk in raw wieners," Lisa said. "That was Ricky's idea."

I nodded, since Jericho Stone had turned his attention to me.

"Two reasons," I said. "I thought that a glimpse of the bone-white chalk would give viewers the realism of a snapped bone. Plus the sound of chalk breaking..."

Jericho shook his head sadly. "That is too gross. Of course, so are the consequences of taking drugs. Who scripted it?"

We were talking, of course, about our anti-drug video. We sat at his pool. It was about an hour away from sunset, and the weather was perfect. Warm, but not too hot. No breeze. No clouds. I understood why so many people wanted to live in Southern California.

"Actually," Lisa said, "there wasn't much to script. It happened because one day, when we were talking about drugs, Mike said it would be smarter to chase a parked car than to take drugs. And Ricky always has to outdo Mike, so he told Mike it would be smarter to slide down a razorblade into a pool of iodine than to take drugs. And pretty soon all of us were coming up with things."

"That's where the idea came from," Jericho said. "But what about the actual scripting? You know, when the guys in the video clip were arguing."

Lisa snorted. "That's how they sound in real life. Always arguing."

Jericho laughed with her. Looking at his relaxed posture and how much it seemed that he enjoyed hanging out with us, I found it difficult to believe that he was hiding something.

But earlier, when I'd asked him what he'd dropped when the rescue guys were taking him away from the trailer, he'd said it was a cell phone and it had been important to him because it held all his phone numbers. He'd also pulled out a cell phone from his pocket and said that somebody on the set had returned it to him.

Which I knew was a twofold lie. He hadn't dropped a cell phone. And it had been stolen from me. But Jericho's warm grin had been so convincing as he told me his story, I was almost ready to doubt myself.

"So," he said from his poolside chair. "Tell me a little about the shooting of the anti-drug video."

Lisa was more than happy to explain. We had acted out the main scene in one continuous shot, with five different camcorders rolling to get it from five different angles. Joel had been holding one of the dogs, ready to let it go when the fake fingers got smashed. Lisa had held the other dog.

We'd used canned meat stew on Ralphy's chest for the dogs to lick. After shooting it in one take, Lisa had then broken it down into tiny segments, getting close-ups of each of us as we repeated our lines.

"The real work," Lisa said, "came when Ralphy and I had to edit it."

Ralphy beamed as Jericho gave him a thumbs-up.

"In fact," Lisa said, "without Ralphy's computer genius, it would never have been possible."

"You know a lot about computers, huh?" Jericho said to him.

Ralphy nodded.

"Know anything about wireless networks?" Stone asked.

"Home networks?" Ralphy said.

"Yeah."

"Bad news," Ralphy said. "Unless you've got it encrypted at 128K or higher, you're wide open for anyone to roam your computer."

I understood, only because Ralphy had once explained it to me. With a wireless network, someone could park outside your house and use a laptop with a similar wireless network to roam into your system, actually uploading to or downloading stuff from the computer inside your house. The only protection was to use an encrypting program, the more complex the better.

Jericho Stone sighed. "I wish I'd have paid you a consulting fee before setting up my system. Must have been a stalker, some fan, but someone messed with my computer a couple of weeks ago. I think I've got it fixed, but it wasn't fun, let me tell you."

What I wanted to blurt out was a simple question: *Is this why all the weird stuff has been happening in the last two days?*

Instead, I nodded sympathetically.

Jericho stood. "But no more talk about my problems. You guys must be hungry. I'll ask Erika to get the barbecue started, and she'll get some burgers ready for us. And then . . ."

He grinned. "And then I'll tell you about my plans for your anti-drug video. I think with my backing, it can be an effective nationwide message. And, of course, it will involve a little money for you guys. If I can get some corporate sponsorship, I—"

Sudden yelling from beyond the pool interrupted Jericho.

"Help! Help!"

It was Mike Andrews.

There was thrashing, as if he were wrestling somebody in the bushes just out of our sight.

And then a single gunshot, loud and echoing in the quiet of the evening air.

CHAPTER 14

"Help! Help!" Mike shouted again from the other side of the hedge. "Before he tries anything crazy!"

Jericho Stone was already moving. Lisa, Ralphy, Joel, and I followed, weaving around the lawn chairs at the side of the pool.

Stone crashed through the hedge, with the rest of us close behind.

A man was on his knees, hands behind his head. I recognized him immediately. He was the gardener, Fred; Jericho Stone had introduced us to him earlier in the day. He was a medium-height guy in khaki shorts and a white T-shirt. Middle-aged, with dark hair and a mustache going a little gray at the ends.

Mike stood behind the gardener, with a gun in the man's back.

"Look, kid," the gardener said, his voice muffled because his face was pointing toward the ground. "Move the gun, will you? I'm afraid you might shoot it again."

Mike looked at us with a shaky grin. "I, um, didn't know the safety was turned off. Good thing I pointed it at the sky, huh."

"You'll give me the gun?" Jericho said to Mike, moving slowly as if Mike were a wild animal that he was afraid to startle.

"Sure," Mike said. "Glad to."

Mike started to pull the pistol away from the gardener's back.

"On second thought," Jericho said, "I'm sure that pistol still has a live round in the chamber. How about just setting it gently on the ground. Make sure the barrel is pointing away from all of us. Hate to see anyone get hurt."

"But what if he tries to get away?" Mike said. "I mean, the guy was spying on you."

"He's on our side," Jericho answered. "A security guard."

"Security guard," Mike repeated, not moving the pistol.

"Well, he sure can't garden," Jericho said with a tinge of a laugh. "Have you noticed—"

"What is going on?" Erika stepped through the hole in the hedge. She wore an apron and her hands were caked with flour. "I heard a shot and—"

She screamed. "A gun!"

"Please," Fred moaned to Jericho. "Before the kid gets nervous and puts a hole in my back."

"Erika!" Jericho said. "Relax!"

Jericho turned to Mike. "Michael, please set the gun down. I'm telling you, Fred works for me. I need protection around here, and he prowls the grounds disguised as a gardener."

Slowly, Mike set the gun on the ground.

"Thank you," Jericho said. "Fred, what happened?"

Fred got to his feet and brushed dirt and crushed leaves off his knees. "I was watching you guys, and suddenly carrot-top here tackles me from behind."

"Carrot-top!" Mike said. I knew he hated it when someone teased him about his hair. "Maybe I ought to tackle you again."

Fred shook his head. "Next thing I know, he's pulling a cowboy move and shooting my gun."

He rubbed a knuckle into his right ear. "I still hear ringing."

"Michael?" Jericho said.

"I saw him peering through the bushes. And I saw a gun in his waistband. I figured it was better to take action first and ask questions later."

"Actually," Jericho replied, "that was probably the smart thing to do."

He turned to Fred. "You and I need to have a little talk, don't we. That was sloppy. What if it had been someone else instead of Mike?"

Someone else? Who? I wanted to ask, but I kept the questions to myself.

"Mr. Stone!" Erika said, hands to her mouth. "I would have never accepted this job if I knew you had armed men on the property."

When she pulled her hands away, they left flour dust on her face.

"Armed *man*," Jericho said. He sighed. "Just one person, Erika."

"Still, I don't know if I want to be here. And my employment agency is definitely going to hear about this."

"Please," Jericho said. "It's just this week while Lisa and her friends are here. They need you. So do I."

Erika looked at Stone, then at us. She hesitated before answering. "All right, then. But I expect an increase in salary."

Jericho nodded.

"Now, if you don't mind," Erika said, "I've got to finish making the cookies. I hope the police don't interrupt me with questions about gunfire."

"Fred will take care of that with a phone call. Right, Fred?"

Fred's answer was to bend over and pick up his gun. He put the safety on and tucked it in the back of his waistband. Then he took a cell phone out of his front pocket and punched a button. He put the phone to his ear.

"Yeah," he said to the person answering. "Patch me through to the local police."

Jericho began to lead us back to the pool.

I stepped on something.

A wallet.

"Hey." I picked it up. I opened it to look for identification. "A wallet!"

"Mine," Fred told me, stepping swiftly forward and yanking it out of my hands. As if he didn't want me to look too closely.

But it was too late.

I'd already seen an identification card behind the plastic sleeve inside.

I didn't tell him that I'd had a chance to see his photo on it. Or the name of the organization on the ID card.

Because if he didn't want me to know who he was, I sure didn't want him to know that I did.

The ID card had had three bold letters on it.

CIA.

Central Intelligence Agency.

CHAPTER 15

"Good-bye!" This was Lisa.

Slamming of the door of the van.

"Good-bye!" Mike.

"Good-bye!" Ralphy.

"Good-bye!" Mike again.

"See you guys." Erika.

"See ya later!" Lisa.

"Bye-bye!" Joel.

"Good-bye!" Ralphy.

"We'll have fun." Lisa.

"All right, all right!" Erika laughed. "Good-bye, good-bye, good-bye!"

"Good-bye!" Mike.

"Bye-bye!" Joel.

"Bye!" Ralphy.

"Wait up, Ricky!" Mike shouted. "Where are you going in such a hurry?"

The sound of Mike running.

"Wait for me, too!" Ralphy began running.

"Well, see ya!" Lisa was still here. I hoped Lisa was standing, as we'd talked about, in a position where Erika couldn't see much beyond her.

"Yes! Yes! Yes!" Erika laughed again. "Go!"

"Bye," Joel said one last time.

From where I was on the backseat floor of the van with a blanket covering me, all of the noise sounded very confusing.

And that was our plan.

It was nine o'clock the next morning, and Erika had just dropped us off at the movie set at the zoo. She'd made us breakfast and packed us food for the day. As she'd driven us into Griffin Park, I had slid down to the floor. When the van stopped, Mike and Ralphy and Lisa and Joel had piled out, taking their lunches and shouting good-byes, all of them leaving on the opposite side of the driver's side of the van.

Would Erika notice that I hadn't left with them?

I hugged the floor of the van. And saw a wad of gum sticking to the carpet just below my nose. I held back a groan of disgust and waited without breathing.

Finally—and it seemed like a long, long time with my head just above the old chewing gum—the van lurched forward.

It had worked. Erika didn't know I was still in the van.

The rest of our plan, I thought, should go smoothly.

The night before, Jericho had asked Erika if she wouldn't mind doing some extra cleaning around the house. So we knew she would be going back to his hillside mansion instead of hanging around the movie set. And the mansion was just where I wanted to be. I'd been elected the one to go back and try to watch Fred, who was a CIA agent pretending to be a gardener pretending to be a security cop. My job was to try to figure out what a spy for the Central Intelligence Agency was doing at Jericho Stone's mansion.

Because seeing that identity card had raised a lot of questions.

Did Jericho Stone know that the CIA was spying on him? If he didn't, what exactly were they trying to find out about him? After all, the CIA was an organization that worked on matters of national security outside of the United States. Did that mean Jericho was some sort of traitor and the CIA was keeping tabs on him? Did it have anything to do with the weird kidnapping that Stone had tried to pretend was not a kidnapping? And did it tie in to the tracking device that he'd dropped outside the trailer on the set? And were the limo drivers really CIA agents, too?

Those didn't seem like the kinds of questions we could take to Jericho Stone. Or to Fred. They sure were questions we did want to answer. If Jericho was an innocent victim of something happening around him, we wanted to be able to warn him about it. But we didn't want to warn him if there was a good reason the CIA was spying on him.

So I was about to spy on a spy.

Erika's window was rolled down, and a breeze filled the van. I was grateful for that. Not only did the carpet below my nose have gum stuck to it, it smelled of spilled soda and other things I didn't want to guess. Whoever had cleaned the rental van could have done a better job.

As she drove, I tried to imagine the van's progress. The road into Griffin Park wound up and down through hills covered with scrub and lined with palmettos. There were horse trails all through the park, and on both of our trips to the set, we'd seen a half-dozen riders on their horses. It was cool, I thought, that such a huge park was set almost within the shadows of the skyscrapers of downtown Los Angeles.

The van shifted from side to side as it made the turns. Then it slowed suddenly. My head dipped down as Erika braked hard, and my nose mushed against the chewed gum.

I was too puzzled to be disgusted.

It seemed a bit too early for the stop sign down at the end of the road, where we usually turned to go past the Forest Lawn Cemetery.

When the van turned left, it felt to me like it was climbing uphill. But that didn't make sense. The last half of the road going out of Griffin Park was downhill, with signs warning motorists to slow down and watch out for horses crossing the road.

Uphill? If Erika wasn't going back to Jericho Stone's mansion, what was our destination?

I was very tempted to sit up and try to peek out of the window to see the van's progress. Minutes later, I was glad that I'd stayed down and out of sight.

Because it didn't take long for Erika to pull over and stop.

The sounds of birds and insects came through her open window. I could hear the van's engine ticking as it began to cool down.

Altogether, it was peaceful.

Until the whining of tires against pavement told me that another vehicle had driven up.

Two doors opened and closed. Hidden on the floor of the

van, I was relying totally on my ears to decipher what was happening.

Two people are getting out of the other vehicle. One on each side.

Footsteps.

They're approaching.

"I don't like this, Andy," Erika said. "We agreed to make no contact except by telephone."

So she knows them.

"We need to talk about this in person," one voice replied. "We're home clear with the first installment. I say we call this off now and be happy with all the money we've got already."

That was Andy.

I knew that voice. The limo driver who had kidnapped us. The same limo driver who had pushed me away from the trailer and taken away the tracking device before disappearing.

And now he's here with Erika?

CHAPTER 16

I was suddenly glad for the stifling heat of the blanket covering me. Now, at least, if the limo driver glanced into the van, he wouldn't see me.

I hoped. Because I didn't think it would be good for my health if they found me.

"No," Erika told him. "We're not calling this off. Sure, the first installment seems like a lot of money, but think about our expenses already."

"I think greed will hurt us," Andy said. "What's left over after those expenses? Probably close to four hundred thousand. If we skate now, no one will ever find us. That's a hundred thousand each. Not bad for a couple days' work."

"And tomorrow's delivery is a half million more. With expenses already paid out of yesterday's half million. So that gym bag he takes to the set is going to be a half million of pure profit of unmarked bills. That's another hundred twenty-five grand each. And I'll bet we can come back in six months and bleed him some more."

Yesterday's half million? What's going on here?

"Let's call it off," a second male voice said. "Those kids..."

"What about those kids, Neil?" Erika said sharply. "We planned it for this week because those kids are great insurance. You saw how quickly he got there in the helicopter for them. No way is Stone going to let them get hurt. If he's a million dollars' worth afraid of bad publicity about his time in the Islamic extremists group, you know he's terrified that something will happen to those kids while they're his responsibility."

Under the blanket, a bug began to crawl across my face. I was already half suffocating, and I wanted out so bad that I was afraid my body would go into spasms.

"But those kids aren't stupid. What if they notice something?"

"Then we really hurt them." Erika paused. "Now that I think about it, that might not be a bad idea. The trailer fire was our first distraction. If something happened to one of them on the set tomorrow—"

"No!" This was Andy. "I didn't sign on to hurt kids."

"It's a little late now," Erika said. "You think you're going to unsign yourself?"

The bug began to climb up one of my nostrils. My hands were at my sides and I didn't dare move to get rid of it. I tried to gently blow air out my nose. That dislodged it. But either it was a stubborn bug or I had an attractive nose, because it immediately began to crawl up the same nostril.

"Maybe I will," Andy said.

"And maybe you'll find yourself as a nice snack for sharks," Erika answered. "Do you have any idea how easy it would be to change your computer records? One quick call, and a pro would track you down in a day and believe he was doing the country a favor by getting rid of you."

"That doesn't scare me," the limo driver said. "The CIA doesn't work like that anymore."

I sucked some air in with my mouth, then blew it harder out my nostrils. Once again, I managed to send the bug on a short ride to my top lip.

"Can you really be sure of that?" Erika asked. "Think of it this way. Who is inside the agency and who isn't?"

And once again the bug made a return trip into my nostril.

"Come on, Andy," Neil said. "Maybe she's bluffing. Maybe she isn't. Let's just stick to the original plan. It will be a lot less hassle than fighting her. And worth a lot more money."

There was silence. Long silence. So long that I didn't dare try blowing the bug out of my nostril. The bug explored high up my nose. Could it reach my brain? I was ready to jump out of the blanket and start beating my head.

"Listen to your buddy," Erika said. "Get back to the set and pretend nothing has happened."

The bug turned around and headed south.

"I don't like being on the set," Andy said. "I'm afraid that one kid will recognize me."

"From the back of your head while you were driving?" Erika asked. "Not likely. He was in the back of the limo. All he'd recognize is your voice, and you won't have to talk to him. Just grab him."

"Grab him? For what?"

The bug crawled out of my nose and onto my lip. I would never have believed there would come a day when I'd be happy to let a bug wander around the top of my mouth. But I was so relieved to have it out of my nostril that mentally I did a little dance of joy.

"That's what I have to figure out tonight," Erika said. She sounded cold-blooded, not at all like the nice, motherly type she'd pretended to be during the week.

Erika's tone changed from angry and commanding to gentle and pleading.

"Andy, just one more day. Then you'll be headed back to Washington with nearly a quarter million dollars. How many years would it take to earn that as a carpenter?"

Andy's sigh reached me clearly, even with my ears covered by the blanket.

"All right," he said. "One more day. I just hope I don't regret the day I built you a fence."

"Never," Erika said. "Trust me."

She started the engine of the van.

Trust her?

Sure, I thought. Just like I'd trust a hungry lion to play nice with a lamb smeared with meat sauce.

CHAPTER 17

About fifteen minutes later, the van stopped
again. I was dizzy from trying to figure out where
Erika had been driving. Or maybe my dizziness was
from the lack of air under the blanket, combined
with the horrible feeling of fear in my stomach.

Erika was not a nanny. Like the gardener, she
was pretending to be someone else, just to be able to
spy on Jericho Stone.

Worse, she sounded very capable of doing real
harm to people she did not like. I would be among
those people if she knew I was in the van. The entire
time she drove, I kept worrying about becoming a
snack for sharks.

The conversation I had heard answered some of
our questions and raised others. But my biggest con-
cern was not in learning more about the situation. It
was simply that I did not want to get caught in the
van by Erika.

Because then she would know that I'd heard
everything.

When the van stopped, I tried to make my body

into a curled-up statue of stone.

But the driver's door opened almost immediately, then shut again.

She'd left the van.

I sure hoped we weren't at Jericho Stone's mansion. The original plan had been for me to wait until Erika was busy housecleaning, then sneak upstairs to a deck where I could watch the property to learn anything I could, then sneak back into the van and wait until she drove to Griffin Park to pick up the others.

Now I didn't dare risk being seen by Erika. If the van was parked at the mansion, I was in big trouble. Already I had to go to the bathroom. I didn't dare get out of the van, but I knew I wouldn't be able to lie on the floor for hours.

That made me remember that we had teased Ralphy when he faced the same situation. And that made me think of exactly how we had teased him. I pictured Niagara Falls. All that water gushing. The sound of the water.

And finally, when I couldn't take the agony any longer, I sat up and peeked out the window.

The van wasn't at the mansion.

Instead, it was parked in a street with rundown shops on both sides. Traffic zoomed by in both directions, but I hadn't been able to hear it because the windows of the van were closed and there had been a blanket over my head.

A busy street!

I quickly scanned for any sign of Erika. I didn't see her in any of the doorways.

This was my chance to bolt, before Erika returned.

I weighed the risk factor.

If she happened to step out of one of the shops at this moment, she might see me.

But the longer I waited, the more the possibility that she would return.

I had to act fast.

The van had sliding doors on both sides. Should I jump out the passenger side? But what if she had gone into a shop on that side of the street? But I faced the same thing on the other, plus the danger of traffic.

Which at this point included Greyhound buses, whizzing by only a couple of feet away from the side of the van.

As I agonized over which side to choose, I saw Erika.

Ahead! Crossing the intersection from left to right. She was walking slowly because of all the people around her. She would turn right onto the sidewalk and come up the passenger side. She wasn't looking at the van. Not yet.

That left me no choice.

I ducked and slid open the door on the driver's side of the van.

I stayed crouched, ready to bolt, glad the traffic was stopped for the red light that let Erika cross in front of it.

Belching exhaust right into my face was the tailpipe of another Greyhound bus. I jumped out of the van and stayed crouched on the street. I slid the door shut behind me.

Then I jumped into the gap between the rear bumper of the bus and the car right behind it.

Had Erika seen me?

I didn't stop to look.

Instead, I took two more steps and worked my way around the side of the bus. Now I was on the yellow center line of the street, with the bus between the van and me. A few cars moved past me going in the opposite direction.

"Hey, kid! Your mother tell you to play in traffic?"

The voice came from above me. Some college-aged guy with long, greasy hair had hung his head out the window of the bus.

The bus began to move.

The light had changed.

I needed it between the van and me. And between me and the sidewalk with Erika.

So I began to jog alongside the bus.

"Hey, kid," the college-aged guy repeated. "Now what are you doing? Going to race a Greyhound?"

He cackled at his joke.

The bus began to move faster.

I sprinted.

"Hey, kid!"

I ignored the voice and pounded the pavement. A few cars honked at me.

The bus was getting away from me, but we were already a half block down from the van. All I could hope was that I'd gone past the point where I'd seen Erika on the sidewalk.

"Hey, kid!"

I couldn't look up. I was concentrating too hard on running right down the yellow center line.

Then *splash*!

It took me a second to figure out what had happened.

The college-aged jerk had poured out a cup of soda. Over my head.

I heard his cackling over the roar of the bus as it pulled away from me.

The only good news was that I'd reached the intersection crosswalk and the light had turned red again.

So I could join pedestrians on the crosswalk and cut to my left and get to the other side of the street of the van.

I got onto the sidewalk and jogged a few steps.

I was in a crowd of people, so I felt safe enough to turn around.

I caught a glimpse of the van, stuck with other cars at the red light.

A few more steps, and I was safely away.

Soaking and sticky, but safe from Erika.

For now.

CHAPTER  18

"You smell."

"I do smell, Mike." I was in a bad mood. A very bad mood. The last two hours had not been fun for me, while here at the movie set, Mike and Lisa and Ralphy and Joel had probably had a great time. "I also see. And hear. And taste. And feel. It's called the five senses."

"I mean, you smell to me and one of my five senses."

"See these five fingers?" I asked. "See how easily they curl into a fist?"

"Sorry, your majesty." Mike caught the edge in my voice but just grinned. Well, half grinned. The other half of his mouth had a huge bite of sandwich in it. And he held an ice-cold soda in one hand. Which meant he'd just made a visit to the food table behind him, where Lisa and Joel and Ralphy and dozens of movie workers were enjoying lunch.

"What I meant, your majesty," he continued, "is that you might want to keep to yourself because of what you do to other people's sense of smell. No offense or anything. It's just a simple fact. Like two plus two equals four. Or that the sun rises in the east and sets in the west. And you are a smelly person right now. Thing is, that sort of fact might actually be offensive to someone else."

He pointed to the movie set behind us. Cameramen and light people were in motion. Other workers were moving cables. "Like them. Nobody supplied them with gas masks for today's shoot. Wouldn't you agree?"

I couldn't disagree with him.

"So why exactly do you carry this disagreeable aroma?" he asked. "I thought your job was going to be simple."

"I wish," I said. "I smell like this because I was under a blanket on a smelly carpet with bugs crawling up my nose. And then I got dumped on with soda, then spent a half hour at the Greyhound bus station trying to clean up, then spent another half hour in a taxi cab where the driver smoked a cigar even though I asked him not to. This was the same cab driver who also told me he didn't like using air-conditioning because it cost too much money, so I sat in my sweat as I inhaled his cigar smoke."

I stopped and tapped my chin. "What else?" I asked myself as if trying real hard to remember. "What else?"

I nodded as if it had suddenly come to me. "That's right. I also spent fifty bucks getting here in that smoke-filled air. Fifty bucks of hard-earned summer vacation money."

"Oh," Mike said.

"And did I mention the cab driver ate raw garlic? Told me he had a cold and that was the best way to cure it. So between puffing on his cigar and chewing raw garlic, he sneezed."

"Oh," Mike said.

"So if you think I'm in a bad mood," I said, "you're right."

"Oh," Mike said.

"And some other things you might want to know," I finished. During the long taxi ride, I'd had a lot of time to think about the entire conversation I'd overheard in the van. "One, Jericho Stone was part of an Islamic extremist group during his college days. Two, because of it, Erika and the limo guys who kidnapped us our first day in Los Angeles are blackmailing him for a million dollars. Three, Erika wants the limo guys—Neil and Andy—to find a way to hurt us tomorrow because it will be a great distraction as they get the last half of the million that Stone is paying them. Four, Erika knows some professional killers in the CIA and she's able to send them after anyone who gets in her way."

Mike's mouth had dropped open. "That's a lot of new information!" he said.

I told him how I'd learned it.

When I finished, I gave Mike a tight smile. "That's been my morning so far. How about yours?"

CHAPTER 19

"I see," Lisa said. Her voice was grim. "Thanks. I love you, too."

She hung up the pay phone.

I studied her face. But I think I already knew the answer from the tone of her voice as she'd spoken to her older brother in Chicago.

She sighed.

Here at the Griffin Park zoo, the two of us had left Mike and Ralphy with Joel in the secure area of the movie set. It should have been a pleasant walk through the rest of the zoo. We'd passed the elephant enclosure, which was scheduled to be part of the movie shoot later in the week. We'd seen the giraffes and the hippos. As usual, the Southern Californian weather was warm but not too hot. Blue sky was a backdrop to the jagged leaves of the palm trees above us. We could smell popcorn in the air and hear the sound of children laughing. Moms pushed babies in strollers, which made me miss my little sister, Rachel, back home. Dads held hands with older kids. It was a perfect day.

Except for the fact that it now looked like we were indirectly involved with a terrorist.

And Lisa's next words confirmed it.

"Yes," she told me. "My brother says Eldon Eldridge spent a lot of time with students from Saudi Arabia. Apparently Eldon's father worked in the oil fields there, so he grew up in that country. He's fluent in their language and knows their customs. My brother says he fit in great with some of the foreign students who tried to spread some extremely radical political beliefs against democracy and the United States. My brother says Eldon spent a lot of time off campus with those groups, and it was rumored that the group was trying to build bombs. But he also said Eldon told him it was just rumor."

Saudi Arabia.

At home, we'd had a lot of discussions around the supper table about the subject of terrorism. So I knew that very, very few Muslims were so extreme in their views that they believed terrorism was the solution. I knew that those few extremists didn't really represent the beliefs of their religion. Just like in North America there were neo-nazis and racist groups who claimed to be Christians but in reality were the opposite.

Saudi Arabia.

But I also knew that many of that tiny minority of extremists had come from Saudi Arabia. So if Eldon Eldridge, in the days before he became famous under his screen name of Jericho Stone, was fluent in their language and had spent time with extreme political groups during his university days, it seemed very possible that he'd become involved with terrorists.

When I explained this to Lisa, she sadly agreed with me.

"Plus," I said, "there's one major piece of evidence that shows he was part of it."

"The fact that he's willing to pay a million dollars in blackmail to keep it secret?"

"Exactly," I said. I continued, "Remember how I told you I heard them talk about splitting the money?"

"You mean while you were under the blanket listening to Erika. When the bug was crawling up your nose."

I should never have told her about the bug.

"Yes," I said, ignoring her smirk about the bug booger, as Mike had called it. "They talked about making four hundred thousand out of the first half million and that it equaled a hundred thousand each. Then Erika said the next half million would be pure profit, or a hundred and twenty-five thousand each."

"And?" Lisa said.

"There was so much else to think about that I didn't realize it until now. Four hundred thousand split four ways is a hundred thousand each. And a half million split four ways is—"

"In other words," Lisa interrupted, "there are four people in on this. Not just the two limo guys and Erika like we assumed."

"Four," I said. "And I think I know who the fourth person is. Fred, the gardener."

"But if you saw his identity card correctly, he's a CIA agent. Why would he—"

Lisa stopped herself as she understood. "Who is in a better position to learn about Jericho Stone's terrorist ties than someone in the CIA?"

"That's right. Someone in the CIA who has access to information on Jericho Stone."

Lisa tapped her front tooth with her right forefinger. "So either Erika is with the CIA, too, or else Fred brought her in on it."

"Yup. Remember how she acted so surprised and angry after Mike tackled Fred? If she's in on it with Fred, she would want to pretend it that way."

"It's the perfect setup. Gardener and nanny. Gives them the chance to be real close to Jericho. Like wolves guarding a sheep."

"Except remember that he's not a sheep," I said. "He's someone with ties to terrorists, and he's willing to pay a million dollars to keep it hidden."

"So it's one wolf against two others."

"With us as sheep in the middle," I reminded her. "Tomorrow Erika wants a distraction like the trailer fire that will let them get away with the other half million. And right now she is planning a way to hurt us to make that happen."

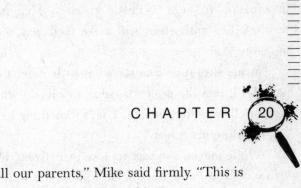

CHAPTER 20

"We call our parents," Mike said firmly. "This is too big for us to handle. Way too big."

Evening had fallen. Mike and Ralphy and I were on the deck of Stone's mansion, overlooking the millions of lights of the Los Angeles valley. Joel and Lisa were inside with Erika, helping her get some hot chocolate ready as a bedtime drink. Lisa would make sure that Erika didn't come out and overhear anything we said on the deck.

I'd already explained everything to Mike and Ralphy, and now we were trying to come up with a solution.

"N-n-no," Ralphy said.

I snapped my head in his direction. He rarely stuttered, and when he did, it meant he was very afraid.

"No?" I repeated.

"If we t-t-tell our parents, what are they going to do?" he asked.

Mike was impatient. "First, they'll arrange for us to get home. Then they'll go to the authorities."

I added to Mike's comments. "Ralphy, Erika and Fred have made a choice to blackmail Stone instead of using that information to fight against terrorists. That makes them traitors. The authorities will make them pay the price. As for Stone . . ."

I made sure my voice stayed at little more than a whisper. "He'll pay the price for being involved with terrorists. Not a million dollars' worth. That's something he can afford. No, he'll lose his career."

"While maybe our parents lose their lives," Ralphy said. "How do you know our phone calls home won't be monitored?"

"Monitored?" Mike sounded less sure of himself.

"Monitored. If I were in Fred's position, with the resources of the CIA, I'd set up a phone tap on the line here."

Ralphy held up a hand so we couldn't interrupt him. "You're going to say we should go somewhere else and use a pay phone to call home. But remember how Ricky just told us that Erika could get information put in a computer that would send out a pro and the limo driver would be shark food? What's to say something won't happen to our parents if they go to the authorities?"

Ralphy dropped his hand. Mike and I thought over what he'd said. The sound of a distant siren rose up to us from the valley.

I let out a deep sigh. "But we can't just let them get away with . . ."

Because it was getting dark, I couldn't see Ralphy's face very well. But I could hear the grin in his voice.

"Who said anything about letting them get away with it?"

CHAPTER 21

"Good-bye," Mike said to Erika. "Thanks for the breakfast to go!"

While the kitchen was bright with lights at five the next morning, outside the windows it was as dark as midnight.

"Don't let him fool you, Erika," I said. "Knowing Mike, he's already eaten it."

Mike grinned. "Guilty as charged."

"Do you need more?" Erika asked. She stood at the counter in a long terry-cloth robe. Her face seemed bleary. I didn't blame her. This was way too early. But that's when Jericho Stone left every day for the movie set, and we'd asked and asked the night before for Mike and me to go along with him. "I can get you another bagel."

"Can't," I quickly said before Mike could agree. "Jericho's waiting for us outside. After the way we twisted his arm last night to let us go with him, we'd better not be late."

I grabbed Mike's arm and pulled him out of the kitchen. "See you on the set when you bring the others."

Erika leaned on the counter and waved wearily with one hand. "Where you guys get the energy..."

I didn't hear the rest of her sentence because we were out the door.

But I could have told her the answer.

Early as it was, we were getting our energy from adrenaline.

Yes sir. We had a plan. And this was the first step.

I trotted behind Mike toward Jericho's Jaguar.

Mike got the front seat.

I got the back.

"Ready, guys?" Stone asked.

In more ways than you realize, I thought.

He put the car in gear and headed down Mulholland Drive.

It was Mike and me. And a world-famous movie star. Overlooking the lights of Hollywood. As we cruised in a Jag.

With a gym bag in the trunk that held a half-million dollars.

Once we left the valley and began to drive up through the hills of Griffin Park toward the zoo, the streetlights were spaced a lot farther apart than before. The interior of the Jag was too dark for me to see more than the figures of Mike and Jericho Stone. Jazz played softly on the radio.

Even though the millions of people of the Los Angeles area surrounded the park, this road seemed remote, especially with no other traffic on it. I wondered what Stone would do if he knew that Mike had sneaked into his garage the night before and looked in the trunk of the Jag to confirm that the money was there. I wondered if a man desperate enough to pay a million dollars to keep his past a secret would also kill a couple of kids for the same reason.

I didn't like those thoughts. Or the lack of conversation that had fallen upon us. Maybe Mike was thinking the same thoughts I had. Maybe Stone was going to slow down any second and pull into a side road and in the darkness attack me and Mike and . . .

To stop my frightening thoughts, I spoke.

"Jericho," I said, "do you ever get tired of being famous?"

He laughed and turned down the radio. "Most people who become famous make that choice. Whether it's acting or politics or sports, they've determined to fight their way to the top. Some reach for the top because they want the fame. Some want the money. Some just want to be at the top, and the fame and riches go along with it. But no matter what their reason, they know ahead of time that fame will come with success. So it drives me crazy when I hear people complain about being famous and how they can't live normal lives. You have to take the good with the bad."

"Do you like being famous?" I asked.

He laughed again. "I think what you're really asking me is if I got into acting to become famous. And the answer is no. I didn't get into it to become rich, either. This is probably not going to make sense, but I really just wanted to be an actor. Always have. In grade school, high school. College and university. And I wanted to be as good as I could be. It just turned out that pursuing excellence brought me to this place in my life. I'm no more or less happy now than I was when I tried breaking into this industry and I lived in a one-bedroom apartment and drove an old, rusted pickup truck."

"Really?" Mike said. "You were just as happy then as now?"

"You guys asked, so I'm going to answer. And it's going to be a serious answer. Ready?"

"Ready," I said. The lights of the zoo parking lot appeared ahead of us. I began to relax. He wasn't going to dump us somewhere.

"If you place your happiness in what you have or how healthy you are or how much fame you have or how much you've been winning at whatever you do, you're in big trouble. Because sooner or later your circumstances will change. No one can win forever in sports. Movie stars get old and other movie stars replace them. The wealthiest, most famous people in the world face the same thing that the poorest, least famous people face. Death. And that's when it all gets taken away. No, you need to be happy regardless of your circumstances. And that, to me, comes from the peace of trusting in God. That no matter what happens on earth, God's got a home waiting for you because He loves you."

He began to slow down the Jag as we reached the security guards and a checkpoint to the movie set. "Let me tell you something. My faith gives me that peace. And hope. And purpose. It's worth a lot more to me than the fame of being where I am in my acting profession."

He stopped and lowered his window to show the security guard his badge.

"Mr. Stone," the guard said. "Go on through."

Jericho raised the window again and pulled forward slowly. At the edge of the eastern hills, the rising sun added an orange glow to the sky.

"I can honestly tell you this, guys," Jericho Stone said. "If I lost all of this tomorrow, I'd still have that peace and hope and purpose."

I wanted to believe him.

Except I knew that the money was in the trunk. Money he was paying blackmailers in order to keep his career.

And he was, of course, one of the greatest actors in the world.

CHAPTER  22

Three hours later, I met Lisa and Joel and Ralphy at Jericho's trailer, a replacement for the one that had been burned two days before.

"Everything go as planned?" Lisa asked.

"As if we'd drawn it up on a whiteboard," I answered. "Remember how we guessed that Stone would look for an excuse to get rid of us as soon as he parked his car?"

Lisa nodded. I wasn't worried about Jericho Stone overhearing any of this. He was out on the set.

"Almost before the car stopped rocking on its springs," I continued, "Stone asked Mike and me to get him some coffee and doughnuts and meet him here at the trailer. So we left, but as soon as we were out of sight, Mike doubled back to spy on Stone. I got the coffee and doughnuts and met Mike five minutes later."

"And?" Ralphy asked.

"And as we guessed, Stone took the gym bag out of the trunk. He hid it under the director's trailer."

"So Mike's been there since, watching it?"

"Yup," I answered.

I dug my wallet out of my pocket. "Here's the money I promised."

I took out two twenties and gave them to Ralphy. "Remember," I said, "disappear somewhere in the zoo. Make sure you're not followed. Don't lose Joel. And don't come back until the end of the day."

"Got it," Ralphy said.

That, too, was our plan. For Ralphy and Joel to get out of danger. Mike was going to stay hidden near the gym bag. And Lisa and I would remain on the set so that Erika and Andy and Neil wouldn't be too suspicious that all of us were gone. But Lisa and I were going to stay near the director the entire day so that there was no way for anyone to hurt us. What we had going in our favor was very simple. We knew who was out to harm us. So all we needed to do was keep a sharp eye out and avoid them.

Ralphy took Joel by the hand. As usual, my little brother had his teddy bear firmly clutched in his other hand. "Come on, pal," Ralphy told Joel. "Let's go have some fun at the zoo."

"Ralphy?" I said.

"Yeah?"

"Remember, that money is hard-earned vacation money. It's just a loan. You will pay it back, right?"

He left without answering.

"Right?" I called to his back.

Still no answer.

All of this was sure costing me a lot of money.

CHAPTER 23

"Learning lots?" Mav Jones asked Lisa. The animal trainer wore his usual black T-shirt, blue jeans, and cowboy boots.

It was eleven o'clock. I was standing beside Lisa, looking in all directions for any kind of trouble. Erika's words kept echoing through my head. *The trailer fire was our first distraction. If something happened to one of them on the set . . .*

Mike was safely hidden, watching the money. Ralphy and Joel were safely touring the zoo; even if Erika could find them, trying to harm them out in the public area of the zoo wouldn't be enough of a distraction here on the movie set. That left Lisa and me as possible targets. But we were near the film crew and behind the director's chair. Nobody would try anything on us here. And I was determined to make sure that neither Fred nor Erika nor the two limo guys got close.

"Learning plenty," Lisa said. "Movie making is ninety-eight percent waiting around, then two percent controlled panic."

Which was true. Most of the time the director and cameramen and light guys were setting up the next shot. When they were ready, the actors would deliver their lines as many times as it took to get it right. Then on to getting the next scene ready.

"Tell me about it," Mav said. He jerked his thumb toward a truck parked at the edge of the set. It had a small trailer attached to it. "I've got my lions over there. We were supposed to be part of the shoot at nine-thirty this morning, and both of them are so old already that I'm afraid they might die before I can let them out."

Mav's lions *were* old. He had to feed them a mixture of mush and hamburger because they couldn't chew properly anymore, especially with their fangs removed.

"Anyway," Mav said, "I was talking to Jericho Stone earlier. He said if there was some time, you guys should get your pictures taken with the lions. Said you might like it as a souvenir."

Lisa gave me a quizzical look. I shrugged. It didn't matter whether we were around people here or around someone like Mav over by his truck. As long as we didn't allow ourselves to become isolated.

"Sounds good," Lisa said. She lifted the small camera hanging by a strap from her neck. "And I've got plenty of film."

"Maybe," I joked, "I could stick my head in the lion's mouth. But I'd probably get killed by drool or bad breath, huh."

Mav smiled. "Safest animals in my collection. My biggest problem is going to be getting them to run when I put them in the lion enclosure."

I knew what he meant. One of today's scenes involved lions chasing the bad guys while they were in the enclosure looking for the diamond in lion droppings. The zoo's lions—which were large, healthy, fully clawed, and fully teethed—would be taken out of the enclosure, with Mav's declawed, toothless lions replacing them.

We followed Mav to his truck.

The trailer behind the truck held his lions. They didn't even bother to get up as we approached. Flies buzzed on the fur of the beasts. It was smelly, very smelly.

"Intestinal problems," Mav apologized as he waved his hand in front of his nose to dispel the odor. "Not much I can do except try to keep them in a breezy place."

A leash hung at the side of the cage. Mav grabbed it with one hand. He searched his pocket with the other.

"Need the keys," he said as he kept fumbling. "Could you grab them from the glove box? The truck is unlocked."

"Sure," Lisa said.

She walked around the side of the truck.

I heard a muffled groan. *What happened to Lisa?*

I made the mistake of walking over to look.

Instantly, a giant hand pulled me beside Lisa. Behind the side of the truck. Out of sight of the director and film crew and all the people Lisa and I had counted on to keep us safe from trouble.

The hand clamped itself around my mouth.

I knew I was in trouble.

It was Andy.

"What's going on here?" Mav demanded as he walked

around the truck and saw the situation.

Neil had Lisa.

Andy had me.

"Step closer to us, old man," Andy said. "Now! Or I snap this kid's neck."

CHAPTER 24

Mav stepped forward. He opened his mouth to shout for help, and the guy holding me reached out with snakelike quickness and punched Mav across the side of the head. Mav sank to his knees, silently, then toppled onto his side.

Lisa kicked backward at the man holding her. Neil just laughed quietly.

I tried to stomp on Andy's toes, hoping he would drop his hand from around my mouth. He dodged my stomp and punched me in the kidneys. My moan of pain was muffled in his large hand.

Seconds later, each of them wrapped duct tape around our mouths. Then around our wrists.

They pushed us inside the cab of the truck. One got in the driver's side, the other in the passenger's side. With Lisa and I jammed in the middle.

And just like that, we'd been kidnapped.

Again.

Instead of driving the truck out of the zoo, however, they went down one of the service roads at the rear of the zoo, making a circle and coming back almost to the site of the movie shoot.

Nobody stopped them; the markings on the side of the truck were familiar to zoo workers. Nobody came over to see what they were doing when they pulled up to a small building with a gray metal door.

"Got the spray?" the guy on the right asked.

"A big bottle," the driver answered.

"Make sure we keep these two kids between the truck and the door," the first guy said. "Even though it looks like Mav's truck belongs here, somebody might have questions if they see them."

Andy got out. He helped Neil drag us from the inside. Then Andy grabbed a pump spray bottle from his back pocket.

"A biological musk," he said. "Think of it as perfume for the lions. You should smell real tasty to them. Real, real tasty."

With the duct tape over our mouths, we couldn't say anything in reply. Lisa tried to kick him one more time, but he just laughed as he sprayed our clothes. It smelled like a mixture of body odor and dead fish.

Then Andy found some keys in his front pocket and opened the gray metal door. And pushed us inside.

He followed, pushing us farther along.

We had entered a small corridor with a door at the end.

We got to that door. He found another key and opened it, too. With quick moves, he yanked the duct tape from our wrists. Then our mouths. The pain was twenty times worse than pulling off a bandage.

"Hey!" I shouted. "Help!"

He grinned. "Make as much noise as you want."

He shoved us through the door, then shut it quickly behind us. The sound of the key locking the door was a small ping of metal against metal.

Sunlight hit us. After the dimness of the corridor, it took a few seconds for my eyes to adjust.

Then I realized where we were. Why he'd driven down the service road in a circle that brought us back to the movie shoot.

Because the door at the back of the small building was the door that led to the lion enclosure.

Where Lisa and I now stood, smelling like a feast fit for the king of the jungle.

And two lions got to their feet and sniffed the air.

Not the old lions that Mav supplied to the movie producer for the upcoming shoot. Zoo lions. Healthy. Big. Strong. And slowly walking our way.

CHAPTER 25

Those first few moments seemed to last five life-times. As time slowed, it seemed all my senses were at full alert. I felt the heat of the sun on the skin of my arms. I heard a distant droning of an airplane. The dry taste of fear in my mouth was bitter. The smell of the lions was like a suffocating blanket. And my eyes saw with clarity the tiny details, like the ends of the hair on the male lion's mane as it began to stalk us.

I looked up at the railing around the enclosure.

Nobody.

This area had been cleared of zoo spectators for the movie shoot. Later, extras would be placed at the railing for the shooting of the next scene. But right now, no one. The director and film crew and actors were probably on a break.

"Do we shout for help?" Lisa whispered.

"He wanted us to shout," I whispered back. "That's why he took the tape off our mouths. Is that because shouting will make the lions attack?"

"Do we run?" she whispered.

"Where?" The enclosure door was locked. The walls were steep enough to keep the lions in. What chance did Lisa and I have of climbing out?

"But we've got to do something."

An image flashed into my mind of one day when I'd seen our neighbor's cat with a mouse. It had the mouse in the middle of the lawn. Whenever the mouse moved, the cat would pounce and trap it. Then back away and watch, tail twitching, ears flattened. When the mouse was motionless, the cat did nothing. When it ran, the cat chased it down.

"I think," I said as quietly as I could, "that if we try anything to escape, the lions will think we are prey."

"That one is getting closer," Lisa said. "I'm not sure standing here is helping much, either. And the smell on our clothes..."

Before I could say anything, a shout from above interrupted.

I glanced at the railing.

Neil had appeared.

Was he gloating? Ready to enjoy the sight of us being mauled by lions?

Instead, he shouted again. "Help! Two kids are stuck with the lions! Help!"

He moved away from the railing and disappeared.

What's going on? First they throw us in here. Then they call for help?

In a flash, I understood. This was the perfect distraction. Everyone in earshot would be running over to see the lions attack two kids.

The lions—a male and a female—moved leisurely in our direction.

I took a small step and stood in front of Lisa.

"Thanks," she whispered.

Not that it will do much good against two lions.

More noise reached us from up top. Dozens of people reached the railing. A woman screamed.

"Don't panic," someone shouted. "Find a rope!"

A rope might be good, but only if we survived long enough to reach it. And only if the lions didn't rip us down from the rope as we tried to climb.

The lions were now less than twenty steps away. Both of them sniffed the air.

"Lisa," I whispered. "They probably aren't hungry, right? They're well fed by the zoo."

"Tell the lions that," she whispered back.

"So if we don't run and we don't smell interesting and we don't threaten them, maybe we have a chance."

"We've got this spray on us," she said.

"I know," I answered, "but I think I have a way to make us smell very unappealing."

I slowly pointed at a giant clump of fresh lion droppings in front of us.

"Please don't tell me that we should . . ."

"Would you eat something that smelled like kitty droppings?" I asked. "All we need to do is rub some on ourselves."

"Some?"

"Lots."

I might have found humor in this, except the lions had begun to circle us.

"You first," she said.

"All right." Slowly, very slowly, I knelt and leaned forward. I grabbed a handful and lifted it to smear on my stomach.

And in that moment, a small *ppphhhhtt* sound passed by my ear.

The nearest lion grunted, then turned its head and bit at its side.

Ppppppphhhhhttttt.

The second lion snarled. It, too, snapped at its side. At a clump of red feathers.

I looked up again. Jericho Stone was standing at the railing, with a rifle in his hand.

Darts!

He'd shot the lion with knockout darts!

The first lion made a puzzled moan and fell over. The second did the same moments later.

The crowd at the railing cheered.

And I turned and hugged Lisa.

It would have been a wonderful moment.

Except that I'd forgotten about the fresh lion droppings in my hand.

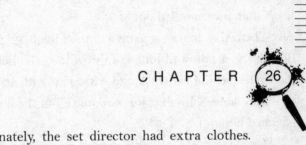

CHAPTER 26

Fortunately, the set director had extra clothes. Lisa and I washed the smelly spray and droppings off as best we could and changed clothes. There was a message for us to meet Jericho Stone at his new trailer.

We found Mike there with Jericho. Both of them were waiting near the parked Jag.

"How about a ride?" Jericho said.

"But," I said to Mike, "the bag of mon—"

"Relax." Mike opened the door of the Jag. "It's all been taken care of."

He flashed me a wide grin. "By me, of course."

Lisa and I hopped into the backseat. Stone left the movie set, lowering the top of the Jag. He drove away slowly, and it was easy to carry on a conversation.

"It wasn't coincidence that I showed up so quickly with that rifle at the lion enclosure," Jericho said. "Mike jumped in the middle of a shoot and told me you guys were in trouble."

"But . . ." I leaned forward between the two front

bucket seats.

"Yes," Mike said. "I'd been watching the gym bag. And let me tell you, it wasn't easy, lying under a trailer all morning. Bugs were crawling everywhere."

Not up your nose, I thought.

"Then Mav Jones came up and took the bag," Mike continued. "So I followed him. He threw it in the lion cage on the trailer behind his truck and covered it with straw."

"Mav Jones!" Lisa sat forward, too. "But the limo drivers punched him out."

Mav Jones? He was the fourth person involved? But what about the CIA agent named Fred?

"Mav Jones," Mike repeated. "I saw him approach you guys. I didn't know what to do. If I ran up and tried warning you guys, he'd know I'd been watching. And at that moment, it didn't look like he could do anything to you on the set."

Mike shook his head. "Boy, was I wrong. It all happened very fast when you reached the truck. I moved behind a nearby trailer, but I didn't see the two limo guys hidden behind the truck until it was too late. I knew if I tried to step in, they'd do the same to me. What you didn't know was that as soon as you guys were inside the truck, the one guy stopped and helped Mav Jones to his feet. Apologized for hitting him so hard. Mav said that was fine, it had to convince you that he wasn't involved. Then Mav told the guy to take you to the lion enclosure. And that's when I went running for Jericho."

"I guessed it would be handy to grab that rifle with knockout darts," Jericho said. "So I headed over there. Just in time, as it turned out."

He shook his head as he laughed. "Ricky, what exactly did you intend to do with the lion droppings? Throw them in the lion's face?"

I explained.

"Might have worked," Stone said. "But I'm glad you didn't have to wait long enough to find out."

Something was wrong here.

"Mike," I said, "does Jericho know why you were watching the bag?"

"I had no choice but to explain it to him while you guys were cleaning up."

"So he knows that we know that he was being blackmailed?" Lisa asked.

Mike nodded.

"And he knows that we know that he was involved with an Islamic terrorist cell during his university days?" she continued.

Mike nodded again.

"Let me jump in," Stone said. He briefly turned to us, then watched the road again. We were well out of the zoo and doing about thirty miles an hour. The breeze felt good in my hair. "Guys, it's true that I was part of the terrorist group. And it's true that I was trying to keep it hidden by paying the blackmailers. But not for the reason you think. The CIA recruited me while I was in university."

"Recruited you?" Lisa said. "You mean you worked for the CIA?"

"Undercover. They knew about my background in Saudi Arabia because when my father worked in the oil fields there, he helped them occasionally. So they also knew I was fluent in the language and the customs. The CIA needed someone to get inside the extremist political group at the university, and they asked me. I spent three years hanging out with extremists there, but in the end, I was able to report back that, for the most part, those students were all talk, no action. That's it."

"But you were being blackmailed. If you had nothing to hide, why try to hide it? And why lie to us?"

"Good questions, Ricky. Yes, I was being blackmailed. I received an e-mail telling me I needed to come up with a million dollars or my terrorist background would be revealed. Because my involvement with the terrorist cell was top secret, that told me either security at the CIA had been breached or someone inside the CIA was trying to use that information."

He slowed for a corner.

Lisa broke in. "So you went along with the blackmail attempt to try to help the CIA, didn't you?"

"You're very smart," he answered. I noticed she blushed. "Yes. I called my contact person at the CIA. They needed to know about it. Plus, there were a few now-graduated students in that terrorist group that the CIA is watching very closely because they have ties with younger terrorist Muslims. If those former students now discovered I'd been spying on them, they'd know they were being watched. It was very important that they not find out I'd been working for the CIA in my college days. In fact, I took an oath of secrecy when I signed on. I couldn't tell you guys a thing about it, and yes, it forced me to mislead you about certain things."

"So Fred is not a traitor," I said.

"No. He's an agent working to help get this sorted out. After I told someone at the CIA about the situation they sent Fred. And all the money it would take to run the operation. Fred came in posing as a security guard pretending to be a gardener. He—and his boss at the CIA—needed badly to find out who was blackmailing me. The unfortunate thing about all of this was the timing. The e-mail reached me the morning you all were supposed to arrive."

"The kidnapping attempt," I said. "And now, knowing Mav Jones is one of them, it makes sense why they took us out to the game preserve."

"Yes. They wanted to show me they really could hurt you if I didn't deliver the money. So the next day I left a bag with a tracer in one of the packets of bills. They used the trailer fire as a distraction and got away with it."

That's when it really hit me. The money!

I tapped Mike on the shoulder. "Hey! Mike! You let Mav Jones get away with the CIA money."

"Looks like it," he said. "It was help you guys or chase the money. Because after the one guy yelled for help at the railing of the lion enclosure, he ran back and jumped in the truck. All three of them took off while people went to watch you guys and the lions."

"Their distraction worked," I said. "It cost the CIA another half million."

"Nope," Mike said. "There's something in the trunk of the Jag. Same stuff that was in there when we went to the set this morning."

"The money?"

"While I was waiting this morning," Mike said, "I

CHAPTER 27

"You called me just in time," Fred told us. He no longer wore the work clothes of a gardener. He wore a black suit and didn't seem hot, despite the cloudless blue sky and the Southern California sunshine. "I caught her just as she was about to leave."

He meant Erika.

She sat in the front of the rental van. Her hands were handcuffed to the steering wheel.

"Give Mike the credit," Stone said. He leaned against the side of the Jag. "Back on the set, he told me..."

Stone stopped himself. "Actually, give Ricky the credit. From what Mike told me, Ricky overheard her talking with the others."

Stone smiled at Lisa. "And I guess Lisa helped with all their planning. And when Ralphy and Joel get back to the set and someone gives them a ride here, we'll give them credit, too."

"Is any of this praise actually worth something from the government?" Mike asked. "Like money?"

Fred rolled his eyeballs. "Not a penny. And, since

this is CIA stuff, you won't get any publicity. This must be kept top secret."

"But," Jericho said to Mike, "you've done a great service for your country."

"Yeah, thanks," Mike said. "That's a line from one of your movies."

"This time it's true," Fred told Mike. He jerked his thumb in Erika's direction. "I fingerprinted her and sent it to the CIA by fax. Her real name is Matilda Eve Buckingham. Turns out she's one of the lower-level computer experts at the agency. I'm guessing that she found a way into some of the older secret files in the computers and saw Stone's file. But it's only a guess. She won't talk."

She could hear us, though. Her eyes glared bullets at Fred.

Fred continued, "I found some of her computer equipment hidden in the house. It looks like she'd scanned your computer, Stone. That's how she knew about the kids coming in."

I nodded, a movement that Fred noticed. I answered his silent question.

"On the first day we met, we were telling her about the video that Lisa's brother sent by e-mail," I said. "And her reaction was that she thought it was gross. She covered it by saying she *guessed* it was gross, but if she'd stolen information from Mr. Stone's computer, it's likely that she had actually seen it."

"But how did she manage to get the employment agency to send her?" Jericho asked.

"Even for a lower level operative, that would be simple,"

Fred answered. "Once she knew you needed a nanny, from your e-mail correspondence, all she'd need to do is hack into the employment agency's computer. Chances are, no one at that agency even knows she's here."

Jericho tapped his fingers on the hood of the Jag. "Well, we've got her. We know the second person was Mav Jones, and that should make it easy to track him down. But the other two guys..."

"Sir." I spoke to Fred. "At least one of the guys who helped her had done some carpentry work for her in Washington, D.C. I overheard that in the van. Will that help?"

"Definitely. We should be able to get his identity that way even if she doesn't want to talk. Thanks."

"You're welcome," I said. I grinned. "Even if it isn't worth any money or publicity."

"Hang on," Stone said. "Fred told Mike it wasn't worth any money from the government. But you guys rescued nearly a half-million dollars. There should be some sort of finder's fee for that."

"Perhaps," Fred grunted. "But we lost that other half million. Erika—I mean Matilda Eve Buckingham—won't say a word about where it went. I'm sure she's thinking about getting it when they finally let her out of jail."

"You mean she could have just buried it somewhere?" Lisa asked.

"Probably not," Fred answered. "She would have put it in storage. There are hundreds of places in Los Angeles it could be. And all she needs is the key to the locker."

An image hit my brain.

"Sir," I said, "I think I know where you might find it."

Epilogue

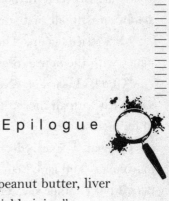

"Blueberry jam, mayonnaise, peanut butter, liver paste, slices of sweet onion, and pickle juice."

I spoke clearly, facing the video camera on a tripod in front of me. It was the Monday after we'd returned from Hollywood. Mike and Lisa and I were in the kitchen at my house.

"No fair!" Mike said. "You're only allowed five things on the sandwich. That was six."

"Sorry." The jars of jam, mayonnaise, peanut butter, sweet onions, and pickles and the tube of liver paste were on the kitchen counter beside me. "I'll take away the peanut butter and pickle juice and add . . ."

I furrowed my brows and scratched my chin as I pretended to think about it. ". . . I'll add chili peppers."

"Cut!" Lisa said. "Perfect."

She swung the video camera in Mike's direction. "Now give me a look of bravery in the face of horror."

Mike grimaced.

"No," Lisa said, "not a look like a bumble bee just flew in your ear. Bravery. Remember, you're supposed to eat the sandwich with all that stuff on it."

Mike tried again. The freckles on his face seemed to dance with the new expression.

"Good," Lisa said. "Now, Ricky, go ahead and make the sandwich with all those things piled on. Go slowly. I'll zoom in for a close-up."

I began. I smeared on the liver paste, then added the mayonnaise and jam. I cut up the sweet onions and chili peppers. I put another slice of bread on top.

"Michael," Lisa said. "Ready?"

"Ready." He moved to a different part of the kitchen counter, with various jars and packages behind him.

Lisa moved to another tripod, focused, then nodded. "Both of you guys are being filmed at the same time. Remember your lines. Let's see if we can do this in one take."

Mike spoke clearly, looking at me. "Your gourmet delight will be a layer of shampoo—"

"Hey," I interrupted, as it was written in the script, "only edible stuff allowed."

"But the label says 'with the scent of green apple,' " Mike answered, holding up a bottle of shampoo. "Green apple. That's a food."

"But shampoo isn't."

"Okay, okay. Then your sandwich will have ketchup, raw egg whites, canned stewed beets, that smelly blue cheese, and . . ."

He grinned triumphantly. ". . . and cat food from a can."

"Cat food!" I said. "Unfair!"

"It's edible."

"But—"

"So you give up?"

"Not a chance."

"And cut!" This was Lisa again.

"Boy," she said. "You guys are good."

Ralphy walked in through the back door and into the kitchen, holding a piece of paper. "Guys! Guys! Just printed out this e-mail from Jericho Stone."

"Ralphy," I said, "where have you been? We're filming our next anti-drug ad."

He made a sour face. "Is this the one where you dare each other to eat a sandwich made with any five edible things of the other person's choice?"

"Yup," Mike said. "Even someone dumb enough to eat a sandwich with ketchup, raw egg whites, canned stewed beets, that smelly blue cheese, and cat food would never try drugs."

Ralphy grinned. "I like that."

"The paper in your hand," I reminded Ralphy. "From Jericho Stone?"

"We're invited to the premiere of *Shroud of the Lion*. In Hollywood. Around Christmastime."

Mike and I gave each other high fives.

Lisa coughed.

We turned and gave her high fives.

"Can't wait to see what we look like," Ralphy said. "I made sure I kept my profile to the camera. I think I have a strong chin."

"We were part of a crowd," Mike told him. "It's not like we'll really stick out."

"I want to see the part where the guy smears lion droppings on himself," I said. With pride. After all, it had been my idea. When the director had heard about it from Jericho Stone, he'd promised to put it in the movie.

"And what about Erika?" Lisa said. "Any news?"

"Ricky was right," Ralphy said. "They found the money. Right where he predicted."

Ralphy read directly from the e-mail printout. " 'It took a few days to get legal permission to review videotapes of the surveillance cameras. But once that was secured, it was a simple matter to replay the approximate times that Ricky suggested. We clearly saw her enter, then tracked her to the appropriate locker.' "

I grinned. Greyhound bus station. Lockers. Why else would Erika have stopped there that morning?

"So they got all the money back," I said.

"All of it. And this e-mail says we're going to get a finder's fee."

Mike groaned. "I bet they make us put it in a college fund, just like every other bit of money that comes into my family. I hate that. Think of the video games I could buy."

"Yeah," Lisa said dryly. "Video games today and a dead-end job the rest of your life because you didn't finish your education. That's almost as dumb as . . ."

We all finished her sentence together. ". . . taking drugs!"

Ralphy was shaking his head. "Mike, actually it's a good-sized finder's fee, and Jericho has pledged to double it if we use the money to promote our anti-drug videos."

"Fair enough; we'll use the finder's fee for that," Mike said. He turned to me. "You know, since Lisa is going to be filming this anyway, I have a real-life offer for you."

"What?" My voice was filled with the suspicion I felt.

"Whoever doesn't finish his sandwich has to cut the other person's lawn for the rest of the summer."

"You're crazy."

"Chicken?"

"Never," I answered.

He grinned. "Hope you like blue cheese and cat food."

I can't say my first bite of his sandwich was very good. Or my second.

All I know is that Mike and I didn't even get halfway through the other person's sandwich before we began another competition at about the same time.

A race to the bathroom.